What others are saying about

A LITTLE BIT OF HEAVEN

"Poignant, touching, and sure to warm the heart of
any horse lover."
—Susan Lohrer, author of *Rocky Road*

Coming Soon

An Eclipse of the Heart (the third installment in the Horses and Hearts series, spring 2017)

A LITTLE BIT OF HEAVEN

A LITTLE BIT OF HEAVEN

by

Collette Caron

ISBN 978-0-9958384-0-6

A LITTLE BIT OF HEAVEN

Printed in the United States of America.

Dedication

This book is dedicated to the memory of my beloved horse, Twobit, whose heart was always way too big for his body. May he run, forever, at the very head of the herd.

Acknowledgments

Just as there are horses with hearts so pure they bless you with their presence, so there are people. I have been unusually fortunate to have four such friends in my life. For the loyalty and love of Joan Fitzpatrick, Lynne Cormack, Debbie Kepke, and Christine Bourgeois, I am grateful and I am humbled.

Chapter 1

UM YUCK

*"There is something about the outside of a horse
that is good for the inside of a man."*
—Winston Churchill.

"CAN I HAVE a horse?"

I slide my mother a look. We are sitting on the laminate floor of our new living room, unpacking boxes. The room smells of bleach and window cleaner, because my mother wouldn't even move one box in until she had scrubbed every surface.

The house is horrible, a stucco box, with cheap floors that are different in every room, and those awful curtains with the hard vertical slats that look as if they belong in an office, but not a nice office, like the real estate office my dad works in. If he still works there. Which, after what happened, I doubt.

The house looks clean enough to me, except for the bathroom, of which there is only one, which totally sucks. The tub and toilet have rusty stains in them. I will *never* actually have a bath in that tub, because, aside from the stains, the thought of other people's naked skin in there just grosses me out. My mom replaced the toilet seat, wearing rubber gloves and muttering about it being the best twenty dollars she ever spent.

The house has that old smell, like my Granny Wilson's house used to have before she moved to the retirement villa. The smell is still there, right underneath all the bleach and window cleaner.

I did not help my mom clean the house. After she showed me which room would be my bedroom, I went outside and sat on the front step and thought it would be nice to cry about it, but I think I have used up all my tears now, so I just sat on the crumbling concrete step, feeling nothing at all, except a cold hard ball inside of me and like I hate my mother.

It is spring, and there is one yellow scraggly tulip growing at the corner of the stairs. At this time of year, outside our condo in downtown Vancouver, there is a half-moon driveway, with a big flower bed in front of it, stuffed with bright pink tulips. Thinking of that, I yank out that one stupid tulip and shred the petals off of it. It doesn't feel as good as I thought it would.

You can't even see any other houses, though I can see the roof of a barn off in the distance. This quiet country road feels as foreign as if I landed on the surface of Mars.

What I noticed out there, sitting on the steps, was that at first it seemed really quiet, creepily so, not that I want to talk about creeps. But then I noticed it wasn't quiet at all. The air was humming, like there were lots of bugs, which is totally disgusting, just like the bathroom. I could hear lots of birds, too, and then a cow mooed.

A cow.

But it is the cow mooing that makes me think of a horse. There is a shed behind our new house, and a big fenced patch of grass with a three-sided shelter in it, so there has been something here before.

So that's what I say to my mom, after she's done cleaning and I have come back inside and we are unpacking boxes on the living room floor.

I say, "If I have to live here in Um Yuck, Nowhere, can I have a horse?"

We actually live on the outskirts of Um Yuck, Nowhere, because the rent was super cheap on this place, which is so far from the maddening crowd in the two-stop light town we have relocated to.

I think the house might have looked better on the internet. I'm sure if they had posted pictures of the bathtub, even in her desperation, my mom would not have rented it.

In my mind, I don't call my new place of residence Um Yuck. Add and substitute letters in the appropriate places and you'll get the idea.

But even though I am a brand-new person, not the same girl who wore a private school uniform and got straight A's, and sauntered by beds of bright tulips, hardly noticing they were there, even though now I am hard and cold and mean, I don't dare say that to my mom. I think she would disown me, and like it or not, she's all I have left.

When I slide her a look to see how she is taking my question about the horse, I see a little bit of hope in her eyes.

Like she hopes she can make me happy.

As if.

I feel a little ashamed of myself, because I know it's all very hard on her, too, without me hating her on top of it. She doesn't even look like the same person she was a week ago.

You know how when you watch the news and something really bad has happened? Like an earthquake or an explosion, and after the tears and shrieking, people are walking around with that look on their faces, that is so shocked and blank they could be zombies?

That is exactly what my mom looks like, since it happened, only minus the dust in her hair and blood running down her face.

She looks thinner than she looked before, and she's always been *svelte*, which is my dad's word for skinny. She hasn't used the blow dryer, the curling or flat iron since it happened. Her hair, which is really pretty, thick and shiny and light brown, is just pulled back into a careless ponytail, held with an elastic band. She doesn't have a drop of make-up on, and she hasn't worn anything but yoga pants and a plain black neck T-shirts for days.

She must be changing her clothes, because she doesn't smell or anything, but she just looks the very same, day in and day out.

It actually makes her look younger, that hollowed-out look to her face, wearing her hair like that, and not wearing make-up.

She probably won't even unpack the curling iron. Maybe not her make-up either. She got a job in a factory here in Um Yuck that makes beer. I don't think you have to wear make-up or dress up to do that kind of stuff.

If I didn't hate her so much, I'd actually feel sorry for her. My mom: who is used to a shiny twenty-third floor condo with granite counter tops in the kitchen and a tub in her own private master bathroom shaped like an egg; my mom who is used to going to the spa and teaching hot yoga classes twice a week; my mom who is used to shopping for five-thousand-dollar Chanel handbags and driving a BMW convertible, is going to be a factory worker in Um Yuck?

The BMW convertible was on a lease we couldn't afford. Plus, we couldn't get all our stuff in it.

So she bought an old van that my friend, Ashley, would have called a pervert van. Not that I want to talk about pervs, or think of Ashley, who unfriended me on Facebook after it happened.

"Oh, Katie," my mom says when I ask her if I can have a horse.

She says it as if it is a *no*, but I can tell how badly she wants to make me happy, and I know if I put just the tiniest bit of pressure on her, she will cave. It is like finding a genie lamp and being allowed to make one wish. But to have this kind of power over my mother is nearly as terrifying as packing up all my stuff on a moment's notice and moving here.

Part of me wants desperately to do the right thing, to put the lamp away as if I had never found it.

To say, *oh, never mind. I don't need a horse.*

But suddenly, I do. I *need* a horse. I can picture myself galloping down that country road in front of this dumpy house, my hair, which is so much like Mom's, light brown and shiny, streaming out behind me. Riding a horse, I know I will feel free, and as if nothing else in the world matters.

"I might as well just kill myself," I mutter.

I sneak a look at my mother. She looks stricken. And I know I will be getting a horse. It should make me happy that I got my way, and that it was so unbelievably easy.

But I don't feel happy at all.

I feel as if I hate myself almost as much as I hate my mom.

Chapter 2

DUNN

"I'M DUNN MCLEOD," the man says. "How can I help you ladies?"

I think Dunn McLeod may be the ugliest man I have ever seen. He is very tall, and very, very skinny. My dad would have said if he stuck out his tongue and turned sideways, he would have looked like a zipper.

The bottom of his nose is bent and looks like it is in the wrong place, and underneath it is a droopy moustache, mostly gray, that brackets both sides of his mouth and just keeps going, right off his chin, like two wooly cigars are dangling there. He has wrinkled pouches under eyes that are dark brown and look weary. If a bloodhound looked like a person, it would look like him.

When I saw the sign on his gate this morning, out the window of the school bus, I thought maybe getting a horse wasn't such a hateful burden to place on my mother after all, but something that was meant to be. Why else would I see a worn out sign, just a few days day after I had asked for a horse, that said, *HORSES, bought, sold, traded, trained*?

I thought about that sign all day, instead of thinking about how hard it was to be in a new school, where no one was unkind, but nobody cared about me, either. This week was the first time, ever, that I had to pick what to wear to school, because I had always gone to private school in Vancouver and we had uniforms. It was really hard to choose, and today I ended up wearing jeans and a t-shirt from the Taylor Swift concert my dad had flown us to LA to see in my other life.

I feel lonely and crushed at school. A few people say hi to me, and ask me if I'm new and where I am from, but I kind of blow them off, because I don't want to get to know anyone so well that they start asking questions. Mom registered me using her maiden name, which shocked me a bit, but on the other hand, it was probably pretty smart. I hate to think what a Google search of the last name I've had all my life would turn up now.

Besides, I have always hated our last name: Lemon, *not related to Jack* my dad used to say when he met people for the first time. He always had a slogan on the back of his business cards that said corny things like: *If life has given you lemons, have LEMON AID*. But I always got teased and felt no pride in the family name. Whatsoever. So, I am glad to be registered for school as Katie Wilson.

There was no phone number on the HORSES sign, or if there was, the bus went by too quickly for me to see it.

But after supper that night—macaroni and cheese—I told my mom, and she hesitated, and looked like she needed to say something, but then she went and got the keys for the van.

Now, we stood in the yard, and it looked pretty deserted. There was a house that looked just like ours—a stucco box—and a big barn, and beyond that some pens with horses in them.

"There's no one here," my mom said, a little too eagerly, but just as she said that, a man came out of the barn, squinted at us, and set down the bucket he was carrying and came over and introduced himself.

I guess I was hoping to see a real cowboy—even some of the boys at school here in Um, Yuck look like real cowboys, in plaid shirts and cowboy boots—but Dunn McLeod, though he walked the way I would expect a cowboy to walk, was disappointing in a worn baseball cap, faded jeans and sneakers.

"We're looking for a horse," my mom said, "for my daughter."

For a moment the bloodhound eyes shift to me, and then he squints off into the distance.

"You know much about horses?"

"No," my mom says.

Dunn McLeod looks at my mom, and just the faintest hint of a smile touches the straight line that his lips. "Well, that's a refreshing answer. Most people who have watched three episodes of *Bonanza* consider themselves certified experts on all things horse."

I have no idea what *Bonanza* is.

"I've had riding lessons," I say, a bit indignant about being lumped together with my mother, who genuinely knows nothing about horses. Our school had *Equestrian Skills* for two hours a day, for two weeks every year, in the spring semester. They are probably starting right now.

You could rent riding boots and jodhpurs and a helmet, but last year, when I was twelve, I didn't want to put my feet into some smelly old boots someone else had used, and I couldn't even think about the pants, even though they came still wrapped in drycleaner's plastic. It hadn't been a problem the year before when I was eleven, but eleven-year-olds are pretty much hopeless. Come to think of it, now that I'm thirteen, so are twelve-year olds.

But to get back to rental riding stuff, my dad thought my new aversion was hilarious, and we went shopping together and he bought me my own helmet, and boots and some snug jodhpurs. I feel a funny shiver down my spine when I think of that, but I shake it off. I hope I packed my riding stuff in one of those big boxes the moving van brought.

"What's your budget?" Dunn asks my mom.

She hesitates.

My dad was in real estate. If someone told him their budget, he always showed them stuff in their price range that was really ugly, and then something great in the price range higher than what they had asked for. He called it moving in for the kill.

"People will stretch for it, if they fall in love," he'd say proudly when he sold another million-dollar-plus house. He was in the Top Ten of Vancouver real estate agents all the time.

So my mom hesitates, thinking, I'm sure, I will fall in love with a horse we can't afford, but then she straightens her shoulders and lifts her chin.

"A thousand dollars," she says. "No wiggle room."

I see Dunn's eyes widen in surprise. I think my dad spent more than that on the helmet and boots and jodhpurs. Maybe she hesitated because she knows how unrealistic it is. She used to spend more than that—way more than that—on a single handbag.

I brace myself, waiting for Dunn to laugh harshly and tell us to quit wasting his time. I'm so embarrassed, I want to die.

But his eyes move to our van, and then to my mom, and finally, briefly, they rest on me. He rocks back on the heels of his sneakers, and looks off into the distance, thinking.

Finally, he says, softly, like he doesn't want me to hear, even though I am standing right there. "Are you sure you know what you're getting into? It's not just the horse. Its tack and foot care and feed. The horse is the cheap part."

I can feel my heart falling like a star falling out of the sky. His words make me see the enormity of what I have asked my mother.

I'm pretty sure my dad doesn't even know where we are, even if he could send my mom some money, which I doubt he could.

One thing about my dad? He made lots of money, and he was confident in his ability to make lots more. Saving for a rainy day was not his style.

And to call what happened a rainy day? That would be like calling the eruption of Mount Saint Helen a little campfire.

My mom doesn't think I know this, because she's a bit of a dunce when it comes to computers, but I've been checking her history. She's become the queen of eBay. And she's not buying stuff, either.

I see her thinking, probably about what she can sell next to make this happen.

"I know what I'm getting into," she says proudly, and for just a moment, she is my old mom, sure of herself, a rich woman who is faintly and unconsciously haughty, so certain is she of her superior position in the world.

Dunn doesn't look particularly impressed, with either my new mom or my old mom. He lifts a skinny shoulder and says, "I'll see if I can find you something."

This should be one of the happiest moments of my life, but it really isn't.

"What's your phone number?" he asks.

My mom tells him, and he doesn't even write it down, which makes me wonder if he's blowing us off because we only have a thousand dollars to spend on a horse. I'm pretty sure we will never hear from him again.

But then he says, "I'll call you in about a week."

And even though I've got a few trust issues right now, I allow myself to hope, because Dunn McLeod seems like maybe he's that kind of person who does exactly what he says he's going to do. He turns on his heel and walks away. We watch him scoop up the bucket he set down and disappear into the darkness of the barn.

It's not until my mom lets out a long breath, that I realize she had stopped breathing, waiting for his answer, holding on so desperately to that faint hope there is a way to make me happy.

You'd think I'd have the decency to smile at her, but I don't. I turn on my heel, just the way he did, and go sit in the van, with my nose stuck in the air, as if none of this really matters to me. As if my heart is not nearly beating out of my chest as I contemplate this thrilling and terrifying new reality that my mom thinks, and that I hope, is going to chase away every other reality.

"Did he look a bit like Sam Elliot?" my mom asks when she gets in the van.

I have no clue who Sam Elliot is. And I don't care. I only care about one thing.

I am getting a horse.

Chapter 3

HORSE

IT IS ALMOST exactly a week later, on a Wednesday evening, that we are back in Dunn's yard. He called my mom and told her he had a horse he wanted us to try out.

I dug out my riding boots, and the jodhpurs, and even though they looked like they would still fit, I shoved them way to the back of my closet, and put on some lululemon pants instead. My dad loved my mom and me wearing lululemon, as if it was some kind of ad for him. Lemon. Get it?

Just like last time, Dunn's place seems deserted, only this time there is dust flying up from one of the pens in the back, so my mom and I walk back there.

I am so nervous and so excited I am quivering, the way I used to feel going to bed on Christmas Eve, but I am trying not to show it.

There is a horse flying around that pen, galloping at the fence, stopping, whirling around and galloping the other way. The horse is shiny and black, and there are flecks of white froth on his neck. His tail is held high and his mane floats out behind him. His nostrils are flaring and it looks blood red inside of his nose.

My mother looks aghast. I am already totally in love.

Dunn comes and stands beside us, and we all watch the horse.

"Is this my horse?" I breathe, enchanted.

Dunn takes a slow step back and peers at me. "Jumping Jehoshaphat" he says. "No, that is most definitely *not* your horse."

When my mother hears his reply, I see she has been holding her breath again, because she draws in a long, relieved gulp of air.

Jumping Jehoshaphat? That's precisely how this town has earned the name, in my mind, of Um Yuck! In what world do they say things like that?

"He's beautiful," I stammer. "What's his name?"

"She," he corrects me. "I'm thinkin' on the name."

"Why can't I have her?" Then I feel embarrassed for asking, because it is probably more than obvious she is way out of our measly price range.

But it turns out, that's not the problem. I wish it was.

"She's dangerous," Dunn says, "Probably going to end up back on the wagon."

"The wagon?" My dad used to talk about going on the wagon, sometimes, but I can't figure out how my dad sitting at the kitchen table holding his head and moaning has anything to do with this horse.

"The meat wagon. It goes through here on its way to Fort Macleod every second Wednesday of the month. There's a slaughter house there."

"A slaughter house for *horses*?"

Dunn nods.

"But why?" I realize after I say it, I probably really don't want to know the answer, and am I ever right.

"Horse meat."

"But that's awful" I whisper, appalled. "What could she have done to deserve being slaughtered for meat?"

Honestly, the thought of horse meat makes me feel sick to my stomach.

"Killed a man in Reno just to watch him die."

My mother and I both stare at him blankly.

"Johnny Cash," he says. "'Folsom Prison Blues.' Never mind, it's probably the same era as *Bonanza*. I'm just saying, this horse has a violent past. Sometimes I can't save 'em, and this might be one of those times."

I could hate him for even thinking of sending this magnificent horse to a slaughter house, but the sadness in his eyes deepens as he watches that horse rush the fence again, gather herself as if she plans to jump, and then skid to a halt. She shakes her head furiously, then whirls and runs the other way.

"The horse I thought you might like try is over here in the barn."

We follow him into the barn. It smells so good in there, of horses and hay and leather, that it almost erases the cloud-over-the-sun feeling of that other horse going on the meat wagon on the second Wednesday of the month. Which is two weeks from now.

Our eyes adjust to the darkness, and I see a horse, at the other end of the barn, cross-tied and saddled with a Western saddle, which I am not used to from our school riding lessons, which are English.

As we get closer, I can feel my heart plummeting.

After the beautiful horse we just saw, the disappointment is crushing.

Since I was wrong last time, I'm scared to decide if it's a boy or a girl. I don't really care, since I don't want this horse.

The horse is small. It is mostly greyish colored but not in a nice way. It doesn't snow very often in Vancouver, but when it does, it is pretty for about ten minutes. And then it starts to melt, and cars drive through it, and these dirty looking piles of sludge pile up all over the place. That is exactly the color of the horse.

Or at least the back of the horse. The front of it, its front legs and shoulder and neck and face, have blotchy freckles superimposed over the sludge. It is as if someone has taken a paint brush and flicked it at him. Some of the splotches are dime-sized, but in places they melt together and look the way a lake looks on a map.

In my old school, there was a freckled girl named Moira, who called herself a "ginger." The exotic name, and the fact she claimed only two per cent of the world's population had her coloring, did not make her seem any more special to me, and it doesn't make the horse seems special, either.

The horse has a scruffy mane that sticks straight up in between his ears, like someone has put gel in it. It flops over two different ways on his neck, but it is not long enough to lie flat, so it looks a bit like straw on a witch's broom, sticking out every which way.

It's the horse's eyes that are the most unattractive, small and squinty. They are ringed in black as if someone has sloppily applied a thick circle of eyeliner around them.

"He's not much to look at," Dunn says, stating the obvious, "and he's small—he misses being a pony by an inch—but he seems like a nice old guy. His name is Lt'l Bit."

He's ugly, he's small *and* he's old. What do I care if he's nice? It's about the dumbest name I've ever heard for a horse, too.

If Dunn had asked me if I wanted to try him, I probably would have said no, but he doesn't ask, he just unhooks him from the cross ties and leads him out of the barn by the reins. There is a large round corral behind it, and Dunn opens the gate and the little horse shuffles in behind him.

I go in, too, in a trance of dejection. I glance at my mom, hoping she will say what I don't have the nerve to say: obviously this is not the horse we were looking for.

But my mom doesn't seem to even know the horse is ugly. She is biting her lip nervously, stuck on the part about killing a man in Reno, just to watch him die, as if every horse now has serial killer potential.

Dunn flips the reins up over the horse's neck, and turns to me.

"Ready?" he says.

I move toward him, just wanting to get it over with. By now, you'd think I'd know that dreams and reality are often on a collision course, and the dreams are the part that end up a smoking heap of twisted parts, like the aftermath of Volkswagen that has been hit by an eighteen wheel truck.

Because I know that, you'd think me, of all people, would not have left myself so wide open to disappointment. Again.

Chapter 4

SURPRISES

I GO TO the left-hand side of the horse, and Dunn passes me the reins. Even though he is so ugly, the horse has a sweet smell to him that fills up my nostrils, and makes me want to just press my nose into his shoulder and leave it there until everything else fades away.

But I take the reins in my hand, and turn the stirrup, put one foot in and then kind of bounce up off my other leg, the way they taught us at riding school, though mostly they wanted us to use the mounting block, because sometimes the chubby-club girls pulled the saddle right over trying to get on.

I am sitting on the horse, and I arrange myself, heels down, reins carefully threaded between my fingers and thumb.

"He's more used to neck reining," Dunn says. He shows me how to take the reins in my left hand and just gently lay them in the direction I want to go.

"Do you think maybe I should use my right hand?" I ask, since I am right-handed.

"You want to leave that free for rolling smokes," he says. I think he's trying to be funny, but he doesn't smile, so I'm not quite sure.

"Start at a walk." Dunn moves out of the way, and goes out and closes the gate. He stands on the other side of the fence beside my mother as I nudge the horse into a walk.

"She's got a good seat," he says, almost as if it surprises him, "and nice hands."

I have to admit his unexpected admiration does quite a bit for my confidence. My mother doesn't say a word, her face frozen with fear.

I walk the horse out, and something in me shifts. It feels so good to be sitting on this horse, even though the saddle is unfamiliar and deep. He moves instantly when I nudge him and he feels light underneath me, a quick, fast walk, almost as if he is dancing.

The school horses plodded along, reluctant. You had to nag at them with your heels to keep them moving.

I feel as if I could just walk around the corral like this for hours, but Dunn says, "Try a trot."

I press him with my legs, and touch my heels to his sides, and I call out "tee-rot" the way we did at riding class. Lt'l Bit moves instantly into a trot. Again, I notice how different he is from the school horses. They had to be convinced to move faster until your legs were tired from pounding on them. When they finally did drag themselves into a trot, it was clunky and jarring.

Lt'l Bit's trot is smooth and energetic. I move into his rhythm, begin to post, rising up from my thighs, instead of my feet. Pretty soon, I find I am not even counting the one-two-one-two-one, but melting into his beat.

"Whenever you're ready," Dunn calls.

I realize he means I can canter. In riding class, there might be one canter, in a ring, near the end of the two-week session. On the very last day, we go on a trail ride, where a stern-faced lady tells us *on pain of death* not to canter at all. We ride single file, in a track worn deep from much use, weaving in and out of trees, the horses plodding along, picking up the pace only as we turn back toward the barns.

I'm a little scared, but I can tell Dunn believes I have this, and even though I barely know him, I somehow don't want to be a big disappointment. When I push the little horse, and call, "*Can*-tur," he leaps into it.

My fear melts into something glorious. I sit back into it, feel the wrap of my legs around his sturdy barrel, and feel joy unfurling in me like a flag that has caught the wind. The little horse is smooth and eager to run, not like the school horses who will slow down to a walk anytime they can. We lope around the corral, over and over, and then Dunn says, "Try a gallop."

I thought I was galloping, and I don't even have a command for this. But when I squeeze the horse with my legs, pressing him, it is like I have pressed the gas pedal on a highly tuned sports car. He revs up to the next gear, and I can feel his power, and for the first time in a long, long time, my own. I start to laugh.

I hear my mother say, as we fly by her, "I have the feeling we just bought a horse."

I tug on the reins, and again, the little horse is so responsive. He falls back into an easy lope, and then a trot, and then I walk over to Dunn and my mom. I stop in front of them. I pat *my* surprising little horse's neck. I can't stop smiling.

"You keep riding," Dunn says. "Your mother and I will go talk business."

On the way home, I am practically vibrating I am so happy and excited. Dunn has promised he will bring the horse over in the next day after supper. It finally penetrates my glee that my mother is strangely quiet.

"What?" I ask her.

"Nothing," she says.

Don't you just hate it when people say nothing, but then go on to say it's really something?

"It's just that we're going to have to buy hay. Dunn will look at the pasture tomorrow when he brings the horse, but he said the grass might be poor, and that regardless, it won't feed him through the winter."

"How much is hay?" I ask. I wonder if *Dunn* is calling my mother *Penny*.

"Seven dollars a bale."

"How many bales does he eat?" I ask. I am suddenly aware of how woefully little Penny and I know.

"I'm not sure. Dunn said he would help me figure it out. The saddle and bridle and blanket are extra. I'm sure I should offer to pay him something for delivering the horse."

I think, *I could go on eBay, too.* Or *Letgo.* I start thinking about what I can sell.

"And then he has to be shod. He has shoes on right now, but he'll need them again in six to eight weeks. It's a hundred and twenty dollars a time. Even if we don't put shoes on him in the winter, he needs his feet trimmed. And he might need his teeth floated, whatever that means, which could be two hundred dollars. He has to be wormed every few months."

"He has worms?" I ask, horrified.

"I guess horses do," my mom says. "Or they can get them if they aren't on a regular worming program, and it can make them very sick. I don't even want to know what a vet costs if the horse gets sick."

It's that dreams versus reality collision thing again. Eighteen wheeler, two, Volkswagen full of dreams, zero.

I long, suddenly, for a time when no one ever talked to me about money or what things cost.

"I'm just warning you," my mom says softly, "you might have to make some sacrifices."

"Anything," I say quickly.

Of course, you know I'm going to live to regret that. But who could have known my mom was talking about the internet? And *Netflix*.

Plus, as it turns out my new horse has a few more surprises up his sleeve. Not that horses have sleeves, but you get what I mean.

But that night, all I care about is that I was getting a horse. And that I need to find a better name for him than Lt'l Bit.

Chapter 5

HONEYMOON

THAT NIGHT, I was so excited I couldn't sleep, so I lay in bed with a notebook and made lists of names. Some of them were funny, because my horse looked a bit like a clown. So I had Bobo, and Freckles and the more classy French clown, with the tear, Pierrot.

I had two part names like race horses have, so Wind Dancer, and Snowy Night and Midnight Eclipse.

Then I had short names, like Rush and Flash and Snap.

And then I had descriptive names like Raindrop, and Paintbrush and Eyeliner. Okay, it was getting *really* late by the time I came up with Eyeliner. In the morning, I thought Revlon might be more subtle.

At school the next day, I hardly even noticed that no one talked to me, or that I sat by myself at lunch. I pulled out my notebook and just kept going with name possibilities.

Stormy. Miss Chief (that would have been good if he was a girl). Spirit. Cheyenne. Dakota. Rumpelstiltskin. I wrote down Gnome and Dwarf and then all seven of the dwarf names. If I thought of it, I wrote it down, whether I was really considering it or not, because scribbling away made me feel busy and like I had a secret life none of these stuck up kids knew about.

You'd think in private school, because of the uniforms, we wouldn't have been stuck up, but we were, and everybody was just as divided into clichés as they are here. I was part of the soccer girl cliché. We hung out together, even when soccer season was over for the year. We weren't exactly mean to anyone else, but it was like they didn't even exist: the really smart ones; and the girls who took drama; and the subsidized kids; they all just floated around outside of our orbit, nuisances to be avoided.

Fat girls were especially invisible to us, but we weren't allowed to call them fat, because that would have been bullying, so we called them the Chub Club instead, or Chubby Clubbies.

And now I'm finding out what that feels like, and if I wasn't getting a horse, I think it would be pretty much unbearable to be even more invisible than a Chubby Clubby.

Dunn brought the horse after supper, which was hotdogs. We did not eat hotdogs at my old home, because my dad said they made the apartment smell bad, like a low class tenement. It seems ironic, now, that my dad would be such an expert on what was low class. Not that I want to think about that, especially on the night my horse is coming home.

My old mom would not have eaten a hotdog, anyway, even if my dad didn't like the smell of them. She is very health conscious, and the Queen of Organic. She had her special places that she shopped for groceries, and nowhere else would do. So, it was *Free Range Ranch* for chicken and beef and eggs and dairy, *Ohm Fantastic Foodstuffs* for produce. My dad used to tease her that her produce really came from Costco and that one of the clerks stood out in the alley changing labels on the mangos from *Product of Mexico* to *Certified Organic*.

She shopped only at Guido's for bread, even though she herself would not eat anything *white:* so no white sugar, or flour. You are probably beginning to get why she is so *svelte.*

But when she ate that hotdog tonight, complete with its snowy white bun that came in a package of eight white buns from McGavin's and not in crusty singles the way buns came from Guido's, she ate it with absolute relish, and I don't mean the hotdog kind of relish, either, though that was smeared on pretty thick.

I know my dad would have thought Dunn's truck and trailer were low class, too. Neither of them had much in the way of paint left, and they were both dented badly. They rattled fiercely as they came down our driveway.

Dunn unloaded Lt'l Bit and tied him to the trailer, and then opened a side door, and told me to get out the tack. He had a bucket full of brushes, and he watched me groom the horse, which we had done at riding lessons all the time. Sometimes it felt as if we spent way more time getting ready to ride than actually riding.

But we had never cleaned their feet, and he showed me how to pick it up, and get all the guck out with a hoof pic that was in the bucket of grooming stuff. If you did it right, it popped out in one big, satisfying chunk.

"You do that every time," he told me sternly. "It's easy to start getting lazy, but don't."

Finally, he was showing me how to place the blanket and the pad, how to put the saddle way up on the wither, and then slide it back down. The girth was way different than on an English saddle, so while my mom watched, radiating anxiety, and looking like she might toss her hot dog, Dunn showed me how to loop it through the rings, then tighten it, and make the knot that would keep it from slipping.

He walked the horse around a bit, and then tightened it again, and told me *always* to do that second tighten. He even showed me a little trick for turning my back to the saddle, and putting the latigo over my shoulder to get some leverage, because I probably wasn't strong enough, otherwise, to get it as tight as it was supposed to be.

The horse actually lowered his head so I could slip the bit into his mouth and the bridle over his ears. We couldn't even put the bridles on the school horses, because they tossed their heads up so high.

Then I mounted, and Dunn opened the pasture gate for me, and I rode inside. While I rode around and around the pasture, trying out different names, he and my mom walked the fences, she carrying a can of nails he had brought with him, and passing them to him when he found a railing that was loose.

He got down on one knee and touched the grass, and I could tell by looking at him he didn't think much of it. My mom found a hose and they filled up the old plastic water trough that said Rubbermaid on it, and he tested it for leaks.

He saw my mom watching me, and I heard him say, "This is the honeymoon. Owning a horse isn't exactly what Mr. Disney would have you believe."

I thought that was a very grumpy kind of thing to say, but you could tell Dunn McLeod was like that, grumpy but with a good heart. My dad was kind of the opposite. He just seemed like the best guy in the whole world. Everybody loved him, and I doubt that people react to Dunn McLeod like that. At all.

But I don't even want to think about my dad's heart.

"For instance," Dunn says, "that horse is going to produce several poops a day that are about the size of an entire litter of Pomeranians. You don't have a tractor to pull harrows, so it's going to have to be picked up."

"Katie, did you hear that?" my mom calls.

Unfortunately.

"Can I pay you something for delivering Lt'l Bit?" my mom asks.

"No, ma'am, you can't."

It seems to me this skinny old guy in his battered hat, and worn out truck, who talks about poop the size of Pomeranians litters, could teach a lot of people, including my dad, about class.

That is part of what is so great about my first night with my horse. I don't have to think about anything at all, not about my dad's heart, or Dunn's, or if I should feel guilty for comparing them.

After a few minutes on my horse, I am just there. With Lt'l Bit's—I'll call him that just until I decide on something better—warmth rising up through the saddle, a soft breeze kissing us, and the reins tugging gently on my hand. I feel as if I have been in a trance, and suddenly, I am awake. I can feel the warmth of the evening sun on my face, and see dust motes floating in its golden orb. I can smell the sweet tang of my horse's sweat and the grass being crushed under his hooves and even the cocoanut scent of the shampoo I used this morning. My skin feels as if it is alive, tingling with something beautiful.

After a while, I didn't really notice Mom and Dunn anymore. And I stopped thinking about names. I walked and I trotted and I cantered. I was a little scared to gallop, because the pasture seemed so much bigger than the corral, so I didn't.

I barely even noticed the light leaching from the sky, not until my mom called.

"Katie, it's getting too dark for that."

At some point, Dunn had gotten into his noisy old truck and rattled away and I hadn't even noticed.

When I got off Lt'l Bit, my legs felt a bit rubbery. I tied him to the fence post by the gate, and took the bridle off and replaced it with a halter. I took the saddle off, and he was all sweaty underneath it, so I brushed him until my arms could barely move. And then, I kissed his nose, soft as velvet, and slipped the halter off his head, and watched him go roll in the grass of his new home. My mom had cleared out a place in the garden shed to put the tack in. She carried the blanket and pad and bridle while I carried the saddle. I was so tired it made the saddle feel like it weighed a ton, as if I would barely make it to the shed with it.

"I'll have to pick you up a wheelbarrow and a shovel," my mom says.

"Oh, poop," I say. I was going to say something else, but when my mom laughs, I'm glad I didn't. If I would have said the other word she wouldn't have laughed, even if she wanted to. She would have told me, sternly, not to say that.

By the time we put everything away and walked up to the house together, it was full dark, and even though we didn't say anything, my mom put her arm over my shoulder, and I didn't even try to duck out from under it. Even though she smelled distinctly like hotdogs.

Chapter 6

REALITY

A T SCHOOL THE next day, I was so excited to get home to my horse, that I didn't notice anything. I worked on name lists some more, and dreamed about long rides down country lanes. I dreamed about being in a horse show, and my little horse leaping huge fences and winning blue ribbons, and me being terribly modest about the victory.

My mom was still at work when I got home, but she had left me a note reminding me to walk the horse after I tightened the girth the first time, and then to tighten it again. Her note said not to go out of the pasture with Lt'l Bit until I was more used to him.

It made me kind of mad, because I had spent the whole day picturing rides down country lanes, but if I'm going to be really honest, I was relieved, too.

I stowed my books and changed my clothes and ran outside. I got all my tack and put it on the fence. I noticed there was a brand-new green wheelbarrow and a shovel sitting by the gate, but poop patrol could wait. I grabbed the halter and went out to catch my horse.

He was about half way across the pasture. I kind of hoped he would recognize me, and run over like a horse would in the movies, but he didn't. He kind of flicked one ear toward me and made me come to him.

Except when I was close enough to put the lead

shank around his neck, he kind of sidled sideways, just out of reach, as if he hadn't noticed me. He didn't even lift his head off the grass.

"Hey," I said softly. "How's my Lt'l Bit today?" I called him that, instead of trying out one of the new names on him, hoping he would recognize it. I moved toward him with my hand out.

He moved away, again, just a little shuffle sideways, that kept him just out of arm's reach. I noticed he was watching me. Could he really look distinctly *sly*?

"That's not very nice," I told him sternly. I moved an inch. He moved an inch, all without lifting his mouth off the grass.

"Stop it."

He gave his head a little shake. It might have been flies, but it seemed like *no*. I moved. He moved. We waltzed around the pasture that way for a good five minutes.

I tried to trick him. I pretended to look off in the distance, instead of at him. I sang a little song under my breath to show him how relaxed I was. He seemed to like my singing, his ears swiveling away.

When I was sure I had lured him into a false sense of security, I lunged at him. I actually managed to grab his mane with my hand.

"Aha! I got you."

But I didn't have him. Startled, he leapt away. There was no way I could hold him with my hand in his mane and he knew it. Still very much free, he stopped and stared at me with his squinty little eyes, wary. He shook his head again. It seemed like a more vehement *no* than last time.

"Come on," I said. I stood very still. I hummed. After a while, he put his head back down, but both ears were pointed at me now, and his sly little gaze was solidly on me. I eased toward him. He eased away.

I tried striding up to him with confidence, he just moved away with more confidence.

In total frustration, after half an hour of doing a dance where all the steps were being dictated by him, I threw the lead rope, and it landed around his neck. I jumped forward to close it in a loop, so I could get the halter on, but he slid out from under it and ran.

He kicked up his heels, as he ran, twisting sideways and farting. There was no mistaking that he was absolutely gleeful to be running away from me.

As soon as he was out of range of me and my halter, he put down his head to eat. Now, he wouldn't even let me get within an arm's length of him. As soon as I moved in his direction, he would snort and gallop—not lope—away. Sometimes, he kicked up and farted. You know that expression? Add insult to injury? You don't really know what that means until a horse you can't catch is farting at you.

And I couldn't catch him. I was now sweating profusely, and nearly sobbing with frustration and anger. Finally, I threw the halter and lead rope at him. I missed him by a mile. I looked around for a rock. I found one, not nearly the size I would have liked, and hurled that at him. Aside from soccer, an athlete I'm not: the rock landed in the grass so far from him he didn't even acknowledge I had thrown it. I found another rock, and threw that one. He seemed unperturbed. He dodged my missile with ease.

"You beady-eyed, stupid, old windbag," I screamed at him.

I'd finally found an advantage to living in the middle of nowhere: there was no one to hear you losing your mind.

"You look like a clown. You are the ugliest horse I've ever seen!"

His ears twitched.

"You have a stupid name! Because you are stupid! Stupid. Stupid. Stupid."

He turned his back end to me, munching away contentedly.

I stormed out of the pasture. I knocked the saddle down off the fence. I went into my ugly new house, and my ugly new room and I slammed the door as hard as I could.

And then I started to cry.

I was so glad my mom wasn't home. If she had heard that howling, she would have known the pain I was in, and I didn't want her to know that beyond the mean, cold face I showed her, there was enough pain to destroy both of us.

When I found the genie lamp, I could have had anything. I could have had a puppy. Or maybe even a cell phone. But no, I had to waste my wish, use all my mother's guilt points, on a stupid horse who hated me.

I thought that horse was going to be like a magic pill, that he would take away all the fear I was feeling about this new world, and that he would fill every empty space that had been left in my life.

And especially the secret one. In the secret space, I am still a little girl. I am a little girl who misses her daddy so much, I think I could die from it.

Chapter 7

FLAWS

I NEVER TOLD my mom I couldn't catch the horse. I don't know why. I think it made me feel like a complete and total loser. Even though I was so mad at her for moving us here, and for changing our whole lives, I knew I had placed a burden on her by demanding a horse.

In a way, I had promised her my happiness in exchange, and I didn't want her to know it wasn't going to work out.

I went and put the saddle away before she even got home. I took the wheelbarrow and picked up poop, which was plentiful, but not nearly as disgusting as you might think. I even cooked dinner, if you can call grilled cheese dinner. But my mom seemed ridiculously happy about it—I don't even think she noticed I gave her the burnt one—as if everything was working out. Why not let one of us have our illusions?

She didn't even catch on that something was wrong when I said I had homework instead of wanting to go out and be with the horse after supper.

The next day, I got off the school bus at Dunn's driveway. I was going to tell him to take the horse back and give my mom back her money. I hoped we could return the wheelbarrow and shovel if I rinsed them out really good with the hose. The price tags had been stuck to both of them. Who knew a wheelbarrow cost over a hundred dollars?

Dunn didn't even notice me. He was in the pen with that black horse. Only it did not seem like the same horse.

Dunn was standing in the middle of the pen. The horse was walking around the outside, her head low, watching him. It reminded me of the way Lt'l Bit had watched me, kind of looking out the corner of her eye, totally focused, while appearing not to.

Dunn lifted his hand, and the horse stopped and faced him. There was no halter on her, and no rope attaching the two of them, and yet it was as if they were joined by an invisible thread. He moved his hand ever so slightly, and the horse turned and walked the other way.

He could make her go faster or slower, just by raising or lowering his hand ever so slightly. The horse walked and then cantered, but it was an easy, relaxed canter, not like when she had been running at the fence. The horse went around and around, moving effortlessly from trot to canter and back again, until he lifted his hand again, palm flat out. A traffic cop calling a halt.

She skidded to a stop and faced him. He put both hands at his sides, and took a small step back, and that horse—the same one who had been flying at the fences and flecked with foam—came into him, *eagerly*, and when she got to him, she lowered her head, as if she was bowing.

And then he lowered his head, as if he was bowing to her. Dunn leaned right into her, until his forehead was pressed against her forehead. There they stood, frozen in that moment, touching each other, tranquil and connected by a lot more than their foreheads.

For a second, I thought I was going to start bawling again, howling, like I had last night. I was going to turn and leave, because the moment seemed so private, and because I think that hope is the most dangerous thing of all, but suddenly, Dunn seemed to know I was there.

He turned away from the horse and came out the gate. That horse followed him like a dog, until he closed the gate on her.

"What's up?" he asks.

"I thought that horse was going on the meat wagon."

He turns and looks at her. She is standing there, staring at him, her eyes soft.

He lifts a shoulder. "There's always hope, I guess."

Sometimes there isn't and I bet he knows that, too.

"I can't catch my horse," I blurt out.

"Ah," he says. "That's a problem."

"I'll say," I mutter.

"Katie, horses and people have something in common. They all have flaws. Every single one of them. So, you have to decide if they have flaws you can live with."

First of all, I am surprised he even knows my name. And second of all, it's not my horse I think about. It's my dad. And my mom. And flaws you can live with. And how dangerous a thing hope is.

I look at that black mare still staring at Dunn adoringly and I realize sometimes there really isn't any hope. At all.

"Obviously I can't live with that flaw," I say firmly. "What's the point of having a horse I can't catch?"

"Maybe the flaw isn't his," Dunn suggests slowly.

"What does that mean?" I ask, hurt, and scared of his answer at the same time. What if the flaw is mine? Isn't that what I'm really scared of? That all this stuff with my dad is really because I'm flawed, that somehow my mom and I were just not enough to fill him? To make him happy?

"First of all, you're just learning, so cut yourself some slack."

So, the flaw *is* mine.

"When I brought him over there," Dunn says, slowly, "you rode him until he was practically stepping on his own tongue he was so tired. So, now he sees you coming across the field, waving your halter at him, and in that little horsey brain of his he thinks something like, *hmmm,* she's a lot of hard work and no reward."

He says it in a way that doesn't make me feel like the world's biggest and most self-centered loser, but just like a person, with flaws, who is learning something new.

"Can I change that?"

"Sure. Next time you approach him, do something different," he suggests.

"What?"

But Dunn lifts that skinny shoulder of his. I want to tell him I've already tried everything, but somehow I don't think that would cut it with him. I know he expects me to figure it out, which is both irritating and reassuring, somehow.

"Does she have a name yet?" I ask him, looking at the black mare.

"I'm thinkin' on it."

"Can I name her?"

"Depends on what you're thinkin'."

"Midnight Eclipse."

His lips twitch a little bit. I can't tell if he is amused by the name or annoyed by it, and I still can't tell when he speaks.

"Do you mind if I just call her Ellie for short? When

I'm training it helps to just have a short name to call out. Besides, I don't want her getting airs with a fancy pants name like that."

I think he is ribbing me, but I'm not sure. "It's not fancy pants," I say, "It's elegant. Ellie sounds like a name for an old plug. They both have two syllables."

He doesn't look convinced, or like the kind of guy who is up on his syllables.

"El-lee. E-Clipse. She's like an eclipse," I say, "Her light was blotted out, but it was only temporary. Now you can see it again."

He smiles at that. "Okay, Eclipse, it is."

He turns his back on me and goes back in the pen with her, scratches her shoulder.

"Eclipse," he says. "What do you think of that?"

She seems to think it is just fine.

Dunn knows we live a good eight kilometers away from him, but he does not offer to drive me home. It is a long walk. All the way back, I think about what I could do that's different, but I don't really come up with anything that would help me catch a horse. By the time I get home, I'm so tired I don't even want to ride. I think I have a blister.

So, I just go in the pasture, and I watch my horse. I notice he has produced a great deal of poop today.

He is watching me, too, out of that sly little eye of his, so I do something different. I don't even try to go near him.

After a while, I lie down on a piece of grass that is not decorated with a pile of Pomeranians. I look up at the sky, and think how blue it is, and how nice the clouds look, startlingly white in all that blue. I think of Eclipse, and the nature of hope.

And pretty soon, Lt'l Bit, kind of grazes his way over

to me, and he eats right beside me. I can hear his teeth grinding away. My mom would probably worry he was going to step on me, but somehow I know he won't. After a while, he is close enough that I reach out and I touch his neck. He twists around and nuzzles my hand. His lips are so soft, and the gesture is so delicate, I start to giggle.

I sit up, and he doesn't run, so I scratch his neck, and he moves his head around so I can get to the itchy spots under his mane.

I don't feel tired anymore, so I go and get a halter, and as soon as he sees it, he gets that crafty look about him, like he can't wait to bolt away from me.

So, I just lie down in the grass, and pretty soon he moseys over, again, and I sit up and slide the rope around his neck and then the halter over his nose. I get up and lead him over to the gate, and tie him up to the post beside it. He yawns as if it is no big deal. I go get his brushes, and I brush him and I check his feet, just the way Dunn showed me.

I talk to him the whole time. I tell him I can probably live with his flaws, even if I have the only horse in the world you have to lay down to catch. Then I go in the house and chop up an apple and a carrot for him, and bring it out on a plate. I don't think my mom would like it that the horse is eating off our plate, because it is part of a set of really good ones that she brought with us from Vancouver.

He eats everything and then licks the plate. His tongue is huge and pink and has black spots on it. He closes his eyes as he licks. His pleasure is so evident it kind of reminds me of my mom eating that hotdog.

When he's finished, I just let him go. But he doesn't go anywhere, he just hangs out near me, munching grass, and looking distinctly pleased with himself, as though he has managed to teach me something, and as if he has decided he can live with my flaws, too.

Chapter 8

BECKY

THE NEXT DAY, I am right back to dreaming. I have spent the whole day thinking I will get home and ride my horse. I am planning on setting up some small jumps in the pasture. In no time, I convince myself that my horse and I will be winning blue ribbons at local shows. Somehow, when I daydream, the horse of my dreams looks more like Eclipse than Lt'l Bit, but that is a minor detail.

Lt'l Bit, it turns out, has dreams of his own, first and foremost which is freedom.

I have my nose buried in a book on the bus so I don't have to talk to anyone, not that anyone is trying very hard to get my attention.

But as the bus slows down at my house, all the kids rush to the window, and are laughing. When I look out the window to see what they are laughing at, there is Lt'l Bit, right out by the mailbox, munching away on the grass around it. I think there might have been a stray tulip or two out there, but he must have eaten them. He doesn't even lift up his head when the bus rattles to a noisy stop just up from the driveway.

At first I think it's kind of cute, like he has broken out of his pasture so he can greet me. But by now, I know Dunn is right. It's not a Disney movie.

And Lt'l Bit is quick to confirm that, because when

I drop my school books, and go to catch him, he sidles away. I don't have a halter, so I guess I just hoped he would remember the carrots and apples and follow me, the way that Eclipse followed Dunn. But no, as I approach him, he bolts down the road after the bus. I can see some of the kids at the back window, laughing hysterically.

I feel a bit hysterical, too, but not in a good way. Aside from feeling like the object of ridicule—just what every new kid in the school wants to feel—I am aware that Lt'l Bit could get hit by a car. Or cause an accident. Or keep running down the road until I never see him again.

Which part of me is feeling frustrated enough to like the idea of. Except that it would be like watching a thousand dollars run away from you, never to return.

I'm beginning to realize a thousand dollars is a lot of money. My mom just got her first pay cheque from the brewery and it was less than that. She hasn't worked any kind of real job for a long time, so she was stunned by the deductions for income tax and EI, whatever that is. She got a kind of worried look on her face looking at her first cheque.

I leave my books, and run to the shed and get the halter before her thousand dollar investment in my happiness gets hit by a car. I feel urgency—okay, panic—but even so, I make myself think, so I go to the kitchen and grab and apple and a carrot, too.

When I come back out of the house, Lt'l Bit is way up the road. The bus is still ahead of him, and has stopped at the next stop. Someone gets off.

I run after the horse, thankful when the bus turns down a different road, so no one can see the horse is running as fast as he can to get away from me.

I reach the bus stop, and a girl who got off is standing there, with her books pressed against her chest.

"You looked like you might need some help," she says, "so I got off the bus."

I recognize her from school. Even though she isn't in any of my classes, I think we are about the same age. She is the kind of girl I never would have even talked to in my old school. She is definitely a Chubby Clubby, and her clothes look like they come from Wal-Mart.

"I'm Becky," she says. "You're the new girl, right?"

"Katie."

"I like your horse. He's cute."

"Do you think so? He's so bad. I just got him and he has... flaws."

She grins at that. "Don't we all?" she says.

I wonder if she is talking about being chubby. The thing about that is that my dad always had something funny—but kind of mean—to say about anyone who was not skinny. Not fat guys so much. But girls and women who were overweight? He was merciless.

"Whale alert off the Portside," he'd say. Or under his breath, "Geez, give the bacon a break, honey," or "Doughnut stocks are on the rise with that one."

Sometimes they weren't even *very* fat, and he'd still have something quite cruel to say.

The weird part of that is, my dad isn't skinny. At all. He's kind of got a belly that his shirt pulls tight around. And a bit of a paunchy face. He always kind of reminded me of that bear that is the mascot for the hamburger place.

The thing is, I always knew my dad wouldn't like me if I was fat. I think my mom knew that about him, too. I knew he wouldn't approve if I had fat friends. Looking at Becky, I can tell, by how she got off the bus to help me when she doesn't even know me, how nice she is.

Suddenly, I don't want to be the kind of person that doesn't even give someone a chance because of how they look. Because they're fat, or because they shop at Wal-Mart or because they eat hotdogs or because they haven't got a million dollars for a house.

Lt'l Bit has stopped up the road in someone's flower bed. He has a bunch of red flowers, part way in his mouth, and part way out, moving in a lazy circle as he chews. I'm not close enough to see his expression, but I'm willing to guess it's pretty darn happy.

A lady comes out with a broom and starts waving it at him and shrieking about her begonias, and Lt'l Bit trots away, with an irritated shake of his head. But he stops and watches her, and when she stops shaking the broom, he saunters back, as if he can't get enough of begonias. She starts shrieking again, and he sidles away, but not very far. They stand there, glaring at each other, facing off.

I know I shouldn't laugh, but I can't help it.

"My begonias," I wail, holding my stomach.

"Stop it," Becky begs me, pulling me behind a shrub. "That's my aunt. I'll get in trouble if we make fun of her."

But she is laughing too. We are bent over from laughing, and then we fall down on the grass and laugh some more.

Naturally, there is nothing as irresistible to my horse as me lying down.

"Look," Becky whispers.

Sure enough, there he is poking his mottled head around the shrub, and giving us his slant-eyed suspicious look.

I remember the carrot and apple and without getting up, I hold them out. He sidles over, and tries to make a snatch and run, but I am too quick for him. I have the rope around his neck and the halter on him before he knows what happened. Once he is caught, he is completely resigned to that. He sighs, and I give Becky the remainder of the carrot to give him.

"What's his name?"

And I say, "Lt'l Bit," just as if I don't have a list with a thousand other way better names on it.

She snaps the lead rope off the bottom of the halter, and puts it on the side buckle and then loops it over his neck and ties a big knot in the buckle on the other side. It is obvious she knows lots about horses.

She bends over and twines her fingers together. "Get on," she says.

So I put my foot in her hand, and she boosts me up on Lt'l Bit. I am a little nervous about riding him with just the halter, but when I pull on the makeshift reins, he stops just as if he has a bridle on. I have never ridden bareback before, and we haven't gone very far when I realize how much I like it.

"You know a bit about horses, don't you?"

"Oh, sure. I grew up on a farm." She gathers up her books. Lt'l Bit walks really fast, and we are leaving Becky behind. I can hear her starting to huff and puff, so I make him get in a ditch, and I call to her to get on, too.

And she slides on behind me, and wraps her arms around my waist, with her books sandwiched between us, and I don't care if anyone thinks we look weird. I say something about begonias, and we laugh all the way back to my house.

Chapter 9

FRIENDS

WHEN WE GET to my house, Becky gets off first, and then I do, and both of us have dirty bottoms from riding the horse with no saddle. Becky looks at the latch on the gate, and figures Lt'l Bit is probably pretty smart and lifted it up with his nose. She finds a piece of twine on the ground and after we have put him in the pasture, she ties the gate shut.

"You want a drink or something?"

"Sure."

She comes in and I find some orange juice in the fridge and we go sit out on the steps and have it.

"Is it fun living on a farm?" I ask her. "Do you have your own horse?"

"I had a pony growing up. We were in gymkhana. That was fun."

"What's gymkhana?" I ask.

"It's games on horseback. Like barrel racing and pole bending. Sometimes there's an obstacle course, and a relay. There's a whole bunch of games and different age categories. I bet Lt'l Bit would be good at it. There's one coming up at the old fair grounds. You could go in it."

"Does it cost anything?"

"I think its twenty dollars."

There was a time I would have spent that after

school on chai latte, skinny, skim milk, and a wheat-and sugar-free muffin, but now I feel scared to ask my mom for *one more thing*.

"I wouldn't know what to do."

"You could look it up online," she says.

I don't tell her we don't have *online*, that I traded it for a horse. "Would you be in it?"

"I don't live on my dad's farm anymore, and we don't have room for a horse in town." She says it as if having a horse is no big deal, and probably, in a rural community like this, it isn't. "I could help you, though, if you wanted to try it."

"Okay. Maybe we could practice and then decide."

"Sure. How come you moved here?" Becky asks.

"My mom got a job at the brewery. She and my dad are splitting up," I say. I realize I have been rehearsing it for a while, in case somebody asks, and now they have.

"Mine, too," Becky says. "Are yours fighting over custody?"

"No," I say.

"You're lucky then. Mine are fighting over custody. I don't think my dad really wants me, he just doesn't want to have to give my mom any money for support."

"That sucks," I say, because really? It does.

"He has a new girlfriend which is super awkward, because she's pretty nice, but I feel as if I should hate her, for my mom's sake."

"Oh," I say. I don't think my dad is going to be getting a new girlfriend anytime soon. He is way too famous in all the wrong ways.

"His new girlfriend is a nurse, so they have lots of money. They wanted me to go to Mexico with them for spring break, but I said no, even though I wanted to go.

I thought it would hurt my mom's feelings, because she can't afford to do anything like that with me."

"We can't afford anything like that either," I say. "Especially now, since I got the horse."

"Sometimes," Becky says with a heartfelt sigh, "There just isn't enough chocolate."

I can't help it. She sounds so woebegone, that I start giggling again. And then she does, too.

"Who did you get the horse from?" she asks.

"Dunn McLeod."

"Oh, geez."

"What does that mean?"

"When my mom and dad split up and my dad got a new girlfriend, my mom decided she needed a new boyfriend, too. She decided it was going to be Dunn McLeod. He used to be a big deal around this town"

"He was? Why?"

"He was a world class reining competitor."

"What's reining?"

"It's to Western riding what dressage is to English riding. It's super cool to watch. They do sliding stops and incredible spins. Anyway, there used to be a sign at the entrance to town, saying *Home of Dunn McLeod, Western Canadian Reining Champion.* He won it two years in a row. But that was a long time ago."

I mull that over, that and the fact that he never told us that he was famous.

"But also, she thinks he looks just like Sam Elliot," Becky says.

"He's old!" I declare of Dunn McLeod.

Becky snorts. "That's what he told my mom. He said, *Lydia, stop calling me. You're the same age as my daughter, and it's just wrong.*" I know he said that, because I was standing in the hall, and he said it so loud I could hear it as if it was on speaker phone. Or maybe it was on speaker phone. My mom had to have a few drinks before she had the nerve to call him."

"He has a daughter?" I say, surprised.

"She died. His wife and his daughter died a long time ago. In a car crash. I think she would have been a little younger than my mom though. Maybe thirty. If she lived, I mean. I think she was ten or maybe eleven when she died. They died on a bad road when he was away at a show. I heard he ripped down that sign about him being the world reining champion after it happened."

I think of those bloodhound eyes and I want to cry for him. Or maybe it's because he said *you're the same age as my daughter and it's just wrong* that I feel as if I want to cry.

I do not want Becky to know I am feeling weirdly emotional, so I say, "Who the heck is Sam Elliot, anyway?"

"He's an old guy. An actor."

"I've never seen him, I'm pretty sure."

"Have you ever read *Wonder?*"

"That's my favorite book! I mean," I amend hastily, "it was when I was little."

"Me, too. Anyway, there's a movie that's kind of like that book."

"Really?"

"It's called *Mask*. It's old, old. It's got Cher in it. And Sam Elliot. But it's really good. I bet you could find it on Netflix."

"We don't have Netflix," I confess, and I kind of brace myself, because Ashley had a way of sneering at you if you didn't have what she had.

And if you did have something that she didn't,

like tickets to the Taylor Swift concert in LA? She'd still sneer.

Taylor Swift? She's so last year.

"You can come to my house and watch it sometime."

Just like that I feel like crying again, so I say something about Cher and plastic surgery, and we talk about other stars who have had really awful plastic surgery and about whether we would ever have it or not, and we both decide we wouldn't.

And it seems so normal, the exact kind of conversation I would have had with some of my other friends back in the day. Plus, Becky likes *Wonder,* too, and I just know Chub Club, for me, is so last year. I think Becky and I are going to be friends, and I know that she would never raise an eyebrow at me and say *Wonder? That's so last year.*

It turns out Becky is a grade higher than me at school, which explains why she isn't in any of my classes. The next day at lunch she asks me if I want to sit with her and her friends, Angela and Marcie. Marcie is Becky's cousin, and Angela lives down the street from Marcie. They are all born and raised Um Yuck girls, who have all known each other since before they started kindergarten.

They aren't like the soccer girls, at all, but they are really smart and funny. They like books more than boys, and we all agree that the book is always better than the movie. No one asks anything about where I'm from, or about why I'm here in Um Yuck, which, of course, I don't call it in front of them.

After that, they just seem to expect me to have lunch with them. The school doesn't have a hot lunch program like my old school did. Some of the kids go to Dairy Queen, which is across the street, but they don't.

They bring their lunch in brown paper bags, just like me, and we sit outside at one of the concrete picnic table under a pussy willow tree and eat.

Becky asks me if I want to go to the movie with them on Saturday night. I don't want to ask my mom for money, since Dunn has found hay for us for us for the winter and the expression on her face when she looked at her first cheque is kind of burned into my mind.

I have lots of other things I could do. I used my last library period to check out gymkhana online and I want to set up some poles and barrels at home. There are some old oil drums behind the shed, and I think I can make some poles. I'm super excited to start it and I should be training to win blue ribbons instead of spending more money going to movies.

So nobody is more surprised than me to hear me saying, super casually, "Sure, that sounds fun."

I knew I could ask my mom for some money, and I knew she would be so happy I was making friends that she wouldn't even remind me she had just made a deposit on seven hundred dollars' worth of hay.

But instead of asking her, in my next library period, I use the free internet and I find Um Yuck's Buy and Sell site. When I go home I dig my old camera out of a box, and I take pictures of those jodhpurs. And as a second thought, the Taylor Swift t-shirt. There isn't lululemon outlet within five hundred miles of here, and all the girls at school love that stuff, so I put a pair of yoga slacks on, too.

It's weird, but I don't even feel sad selling stuff from my old life. Nobody buys anything in time for the movie, so I ask Becky if maybe we could watch *Mask* at her place instead.

She doesn't even ask me why, she's just really cool

about it, and that's what we do. Her mom is on her way to work, which is a shift at the 7-Eleven. She is plump, like Becky, but really pretty. She's one of those outgoing people who laughs loud and flips her hair around. I bet she slaps people on the arm when she talks to them.

The house is ugly, just like mine, and the fixtures in the bathroom have the same stains in them as ours. I find out it's because lots of houses are on wells and there is too much iron in the water.

I like it at Becky's. You don't have to worry about finger prints or knocking over the Lalique vase. Angela and Marcie come, too, and even though it's not like, say, at Ashley's house in English Bay, where you do have to worry about fingerprints and the Lalique vase, it reminds me of my old life, especially when we start giggling about Sam Elliot and how ridiculously old he must be *now* since the movie, *Mask,* is ancient.

Speaking of my old life, my grandma phones us a week or so after I've been to Becky's for the movie. Not my mom's mom, Granny Wilson, who lives in the retirement villa in Vancouver, but my dad's mom, Grandma Lemon, who lives in Ottawa.

My mom is baking cookies, which is very different because she has never been the cookie baking kind of mom. At all. I think she might be trying to save money on our lunches.

Anyway, she presses her phone close to her ear, as if to protect me from the fact my grandma is yelling at her, which is not cool, because even though it's okay for me to be mad at my mom, it's not okay for anyone else.

My mom finally says she has to go, and then hesitates and hands the phone to me.

My grandma, who was just screaming at my mom so loud I could hear her, puts on a sweet soft voice for me. She says my dad really misses me and she is sorry my mom was so hasty and ripped me away from everything I knew and from a father who loved me so much, and who has been unfairly accused of things—entrapped—and would soon be vindicated in a court of law. And do I know that he has a right to see me? That nothing has been proven? And that, *of course,* nothing will be proven?

Then she asks me, super casually, what I said to the police when they talked to me.

I tell her the truth. Nothing. There was nothing to say. It wasn't actually the police who talked to me, it was a social worker, but I doubt my grandmother is interested in the distinction.

Even though my Grandma is using her nicey-nice voice, I can tell she is really, really angry. She asks where we are living, and I say, *oh, grandma, I have to go, the cookies are burning.* Which they are.

I don't want my dad showing up here. Even if he does have a right to see me. Maybe especially if he has a *right* to see me.

I wonder why he didn't phone himself if he loves me so much and obviously if my grandparents could find the number even though my mom got a new phone the day we got here, so could my dad.

After I disconnect, I feel so sad. My grandma never even asked about *me.* I didn't even get a chance to tell her about my horse, or my new friend. When the phone starts ringing again, and my mom looks at the caller ID and just shuts it off and puts it in her pocket, I feel exactly like those burned cookies that my mom pulls out of the oven and looks at. Damaged, somehow.

I feel as if I don't know what's true about anyone, anymore. My grandmother and grandfather, on my dad's side, are super nice. They have a place in "cottage country" which is on Lake Muskoka.

My Grandpa Lemon likes to point out there are even chairs named after *his* lake, and people who call them Adirondack chairs are just plain dumb. Or American. Anyway, we go to "cottage country" every year for a week in the summer. The cottage is very old and has a name, *Sunnyside,* and has been in the Lemon family for about a hundred years.

The whole week is so much fun. We swim and play board games and have bonfires at night and make s'mores. I remember the first time I swam all the way out to the raft, when I was seven, and how happy and proud and scared I was.

I never knew how dark it could get at night, or how gorgeous the stars looked in the summer sky until we were at Sunnyside.

All year long, when it's not summer, we did Skype or Facetime nearly every week and my Grandpa Lemon was hilarious, putting his hand in a sock and calling it Jose. Jose pronounced my name Cat-ee and always had some super corny jokes to tell me, like *Cat-ee do you know what cannoli is? Millie,* (that's my grandma's name) *I cannoli do one thing at a time.* My Grandpa doesn't even talk to me today. I don't know if it's because I hung up too soon, or because he doesn't want to.

I wonder if we will go to the cottage this summer, but I'm pretty sure I already know the answer. I wonder if I will ever go to the cottage again.

My mom is turning the cookies over to see if she can rescue any of them, but she looks pale and shaken, I don't feel like cookies anymore. I go outside, and Lt'l Bit comes over to the fence to check and see if I have an apple for him, which I do.

I hold it flat in the palm of my hand, and he takes a bite, but he doesn't chew it. He holds it in his mouth, and sucks on it, loudly. His eyes close to little squints of perfect contentment. If I wasn't crying, I might laugh. I feed him the rest of the apple, and he eats the whole thing that way, holding it in his mouth and sucking all the juice out before he finally chews it. It takes him about fifteen minutes to eat the apple. Then I go get his halter, and even though he's already eaten his apple, he decides to be nice and let me catch him. I don't feel like practicing for the gymkhana now, so I just brush him and tell him all my woes, of which there seems to be many.

His little slant eye never leaves me the whole time. He even nods his head up and down a couple of times, which could mean *I totally get you* but probably it means I missed a spot.

I am out there, and it is nearly dark, when Dunn pulls in and backs a trailer full of hay up to the shed.

I know he didn't have to bring the hay, or help us find any, either. My mom doesn't think I know this, but she is making twenty-dollar payments on the tack, which he also found for us. It strikes me as really weird, that Dunn, who hardly knows us, is helping us, and my Grandma and Grandpa Lemon, who my mom has treated like her own parents for fifteen years, didn't only *not* ask about me, but didn't ask if we needed anything or if we are okay.

That doesn't seem like love to me, but contemplating love, and how it really works and who really loves me, makes me feel as if I'm quaking inside, like a tsunami is about to hit.

I watch Dunn lift his nose to the air, and say, "What's burning?" I feel really glad that he is here. Dunn makes me feel as if, even if a tsunami hits, the world has safe places in it.

"My mom burned cookies," I say.

He squints through the deepening dusk at me, and goes and takes the straps off the hay, and says, uncomfortably, as he starts to move it, one bale at a time, "You crying over burnt cookies or did your best buddy there stand on your toe?"

And I never thought I would say this to a single living person, but I say to Dunn McLeod, "Do you know what a Chester Catcher is?"

I think I say it to him because of what Becky said. That he wouldn't date her mother because she was the same age his daughter would have been, if she hadn't died.

Chapter 10

LOVE

DUNN DOESN'T STOP moving hay, but he seems to be mulling that over. "A Chester Catcher? Like a chesterfield?"

"No," I say. "Not like that. At all."

The first hint I had that my life was about to change was when Janey Nelson came up to me at my old school. She wasn't someone I talked to very much, a Chub Club girl whose uniform always looked sloppy and who had the worst hair—think Donald Trump, only brown.

It wasn't that I wasn't nice to her. She just didn't really exist in my world.

I didn't like the look on her face when she came up to me, kind of a mean smile, as if she didn't like *me*.

"I saw your dad on TV last night," she said.

I was at my locker and I kind of glanced at her, and snorted. "My dad wasn't on TV last night."

"I didn't see his face, but I recognized his tie. The one with the cartoon dragons on it."

My dad had this thing: his trademark, he called it. He wore really good suits, like Armani and Hugo Boss, but he always wore a playful, unique tie. His tie collection made it fun and easy to shop for him for his birthday and Christmas.

He had lots of ties with lemons on them, and he had a tie with rows of purple houses on it, and lots of ties with cartoon characters, like the dragon one that Janey is talking about. My favorite is one my mom and I found for him in Disneyland with Eeyore on it. I wanted to give it to him right away, as soon as we bought it, but my mom made me save it for him for his birthday. His face lit up like he had made a five-million-dollar sale when he saw that tie.

"My dad wasn't on TV last night," I told Janey, closing my locker firmly, and turning away from her without even giving her another look. "Lots of people have ties like that."

"I doubt that," she said snippily, and it turned out she was right, and that stupidly, I was glad he was wearing the dragon tie that night and not the Eeyore one.

"So are you gonna tell me?" Dunn says, "Or leave me in suspense?"

That moment when I wanted to tell him has evaporated. I think of the anger in my Grandma Lemon's voice, and her saying my dad has been unfairly accused. I suddenly feel ashamed of myself that I almost told him anything about my dad, like it is a deep, dark secret that I better keep to myself.

"I'll leave you in suspense," I say, but then I add, "Or you can look on the internet."

"I don't have the internet, so I guess when you're ready, you'll tell me. Or not. Either way is okay with me."

He doesn't say it like he doesn't care. He says it like he *respects* me and thinks I will make the right choice. I think I told him to look on the internet because I wanted him to know, but not to know from me. Why would I feel as if I was betraying my dad, when it is the other way around? Maybe because of talking to Grandma Lemon.

"Let's go see about those cookies," he says.

"They're burnt."

"That doesn't matter one little bit to a man who hasn't had a homemade cookie in about twenty years."

It makes me realize he probably hasn't had a homemade cookie since his wife died. Is it wrong to like it that other people have sorrows?

I let Lt'l Bit go, and follow Dunn toward the house. We are nearly there when we see the silver cookie trays lying, upside down, in the grass where my mom threw them. There are cookies scattered all around them, the ones that fell bottom up are pretty black.

Dunn doesn't even hesitate. He picks one of those black-bottomed cookies out of the grass and starts to munch on it.

The expression on his face is so much like Lt'l Bit's was, eating the apple, that I start to laugh, even though just a few minutes ago, with that tsunami-about-to-hit feeling inside of me, it felt like I might never laugh again.

"Mighty fine cookies, Penny," he calls.

"You're a desperate man," she calls back, and she comes out the screen door and lets it slap shut behind her. The light is shining from behind her.

I don't remember if she was wearing that dress before, but she has on a summer dress, and her shoulders and her feet and her legs are bare. It is hot here in Um Yuck. We are not used to hot weather. Vancouver is notoriously wet and cool.

I hope that is why she has put on this dress. Her hair is tied back, and she is flushed, I hope from the heat of the oven, though I am uncomfortably aware, my mother is looking at Dunn McLeod as if he is Sam Elliot.

And I wouldn't like it one bit, except I know something about Dunn McLeod that she doesn't.

She looks about nineteen, which she isn't, but he

is not interested in people her age, which is thirty-six, nearly the very same as Becky's mom, Lydia.

He untucks his shirt, and makes a kind of basket with the shirttails, and wanders around in the dark searching for cookies as if he is on an Easter egg hunt.

When his shirt is bulging with cookies, he turns back to his truck, and waves a casual hand at us, and we watch him get in it, organize his cookies on the seat beside him, and drive away.

My mom sits down on the stairs, and rests her hand in her chin, and I sit down beside her. The night is warm and full of sounds I would have never heard in Vancouver. I can hear crickets, and a frog, and far away, the hoot of an owl.

"Do you like Dunn?" I ask my mom.

"Of course," she says, and I like the way she says it, the same way she would say it if I asked her if she liked Mrs. Beckett who was our next door neighbor in Vancouver.

She seems to realize the question is loaded, and she says, "Not like that."

I am unbelievably relieved by that. "That's good," I say. "He's very old."

She actually laughs. "How old do you think he is?"

"About a hundred," I say, though I realize I don't really think that. He lifted those bales with ease, as if they didn't weigh anything, and I know they weigh about sixty pounds each. My Grandpa Lemon, who is seventy-one, could have never lifted a bale like that. But probably not when he was thirty, either. He always worked in an office for the government.

"I think he's probably in his fifties."

"Old," I agree.

"Katie, I'm not even divorced from your dad yet. I

have a lot of things to figure out, and the only thing that really matters to me is making good decisions so I can make a great life for you, despite everything that has happened. A romantic interest is not even part of that equation."

I feel so relieved. Dunn doesn't like my mom, *that way,* and she doesn't like him *that way* either.

It is full dark and the night is inky black, beaded with stars that look like the diamond stud earrings my dad gave my mom on their tenth anniversary. I am pretty sure my mom sold them last week on eBay.

Who would have believed this? The night sky in Um Yuck can be every bit as pretty as it ever was in Lake Muskoka?

"We could probably have a fire pit here," I say. I can already picture Becky and me pulling blackened marshmallows off sticks.

"Yes, we probably could," my mother says.

And all those burning questions I had about love just seem to fade away when she puts her arm around my shoulder, and uses her other hand to smooth my hair.

Chapter 11

GYMKHANA

SOME OF MY stuff sells on the Um Yuck Buy and Sell, so I have my own money for the gymkhana entry fee, which you have to pay a week in advance so that they know how many people will be in it, and in what age groups.

It is Becky who tells me that, and Becky who helps me get ready. We carefully measure where to put each barrel, ninety feet between the one barrel and the two barrel, and one hundred and five feet between one and three and two and three. I have the poles set up, six of them, 21 feet apart down one side of the pasture.

Her dad makes me the poles, out of PVC pipe and milk jugs filled with sand, because the ones I tried to make were a disaster. This is without even meeting me, yet, which makes me think he is maybe not as big a jerk as Becky thinks he is. He has offered to come get me and Lt'l Bit for the gymkhana, because the ride to the fairgrounds would be so long that Lt'l Bit would be worn out before we got there. I almost say no, even after all the work we've done, because I don't want to be alone with a strange man in the cab of his truck, but then Becky tells me she is going to stay overnight with him on the Friday before the Saturday gymkhana, so she'll be with him.

She comes over almost every night and helps me

practice. She is hilarious. She puts on her "coach" hat, which is a purple toque that actually says *coach* on it, not the kind of Coach my mother used to like and is now selling like crazy. She has a stop watch and everything. She jumps up and down every time I shave even part of a second off.

Lt'l Bit is like the wonder horse when we practice. He can usually do that cloverleaf pattern around the barrels in about twenty seconds. Becky thinks he's probably done all this before. Which means somebody else loved him once, almost as much as I do. But then how did they let him go? How can that feeling called love be one thing one day, and something totally different the next?

One thing I've noticed about Um Yuck is that the kids here are mostly rural and they are not really sentimental about animals. They are more pragmatic, like an animal is a tool to be used. Even Becky is a bit like that.

Still, I plan to ask Dunn, the next time I see him, if he knows where Lt'l Bit came from.

I can't sleep the night before the gymkhana, and I am up early, before it is even light out, braid my hair and put a pink ribbon in the braid. Then I brush Lt'l Bit and braid his scanty mane with the same pink ribbon. My mom is so upset because she has to work, and won't be able to see me in my first gymkhana. She has given me her cell phone and made me promise to have Becky video every second of it.

I am entered in four events: 13- to 16-year-old poles, barrels, obstacle, and relay. For the relay they put you teams of four with complete strangers and you have to carry a spoon with an egg on it across the arena and pass it to your team mate. Becky said it can be the most fun part of the whole day.

Becky has made me practice carrying an egg in a spoon while riding. After I went through a dozen eggs, splattering them all over the place, my mom boiled some for me to use.

We have also set up an obstacle course, but Becky said you never know what they might throw into it. There is usually a gate you have to open and shut, without getting off the horse, and there is usually a bridge you have to cross. We don't know how to build a bridge, or where there is one we can practice on, so we'll just keep our fingers crossed about that.

Becky and her dad arrive right when they said they would, which is good because I would have been a wreck if they were late. I already caught Lt'l Bit two hours early just in case he got it in his head to be difficult today of all days.

Becky's dad's truck and trailer are quite a bit nicer than Dunn's are and both have bright signs on them that say *Meadowbrook Farms.*

He seems like a nice guy. When Becky introduces me, he shakes my hand, which makes me feel very grown up. You can tell from the way he handles Lt'l Bit he has been around livestock his whole life.

Becky is wearing her *coach* toque, even though it's supposed to be really hot today. She looks as nervous as I feel! We all crowd onto the front seat of the truck, her beside her dad in the middle seat, and I can feel her shoulder shaking when it touches mine.

The gymkhana is not as big as I thought it would be. It is held on the fair grounds. There is an outdoor arena with an announcer's stand, and some bleachers on one side of it. There are only about three or four dozen people in the bleachers.

After you sign in, you get your horse ready, and

then you can ride around an old race track that goes all the way around the arena.

There are maybe a total of twenty-one or twenty-two kids there in four different age categories. I go stand Lt'l Bit beside Becky to watch when it starts.

The really little kids start, five of them, on adorable but horrible little ponies who basically do whatever they want. When the one little pony lies down and his rider, who looks about three, has to jump off while the pony rolls around in the dust, Becky and I laugh so hard that we forget to be nervous.

But then the next age group comes out, which means it is time for me to warm up. They say horses can sense how you are feeling, but Lt'l Bit doesn't seem to have a clue how nervous I am, or to be bothered by the loud speaker system. In fact, when I am mounted, and adjusting my helmet, he gives his head a shake and yawns mightily.

Two girls, about my age, ride over to us. Their horses are huge, and all muscled up and gleaming. One's horse is light brown and the other's is dark brown. The horses seem all wired up, and neither of them will stand still, prancing sideways.

"That's a funny looking horse," one of the girls says to me.

It's been so long since I thought of my horse as funny looking that I am shocked. I don't know what to say, so I just kind of hunker down in the saddle.

"I sure hope he can run," the taller of the two girls says, and they both snicker.

Becky is suddenly there, arms folded over her chest. "Oh, he can run," she says.

The girls move off, putting those horses into easy lopes around the track that surrounds the arena.

Becky watches them with narrowed eyes. "Rich girls," she says. "They're from Pleasant Valley, which is the next town north of here. I heard Rhonda's dad paid thirty thousand dollars for that quarter horse mare."

"Which one is Rhonda?"

"The blonde one on the darker horse. The other one is Lacey. That's a really expensive horse, too. It's a retired reining horse."

I watch Lacey and Rhonda ride, rich and sure of their privilege, and I think *that used to be me*. Minus a thirty-thousand-dollar horse, but me just the same.

They call our category, and barrels are first. There are seven girls in my category.

Lacey rides first, but all that confidence she had loping around the outer track is gone.

Becky is grinning ear to ear when her run is finished. "Her time sucks," she says happily, when they call it as twenty-one point five.

Another girl goes next, but knocks over a barrel, which gives her a five second penalty and probably puts her out of the running.

Now it is Lt'l Bit's turn. I ride into the arena, and he turns into a different horse. He is prancing hard, and tossing his head and pulling against the bit as we wait behind the red line. He is doing this thing where he rears up slightly on his back legs and then pops back down, hard, on his front ones. I've never seen him like this and I am scared stiff.

The starting horn goes off, and without any signal from me, he blasts across the red line like a ball out of a cannon. He hits the first barrel, and it makes a booming noise. He surges around it. We have practiced with metal ones, but this one is plastic and much lighter, and out of the corner of my eye, I see it go down.

I have no control over him. Even when I galloped him, that first time at Dunn's, he was not going like this. When I have practiced at home, he has done a nice controlled lope through the cloverleaf pattern. But now, he hits the second barrel harder than the first one and it goes down, too. I know we can't win, but at this point I am feeling as if I will be happy to survive. I am wrestling with the bit, trying to get him to slow down, but he won't. He knocks over the third barrel, too, and I hear the announcer say I am disqualified.

Lt'l Bit doesn't care. He just charges toward the finish line, skids to a halt at the closed gate, and stands there huffing and puffing.

Becky opens the gate for me and I walk Lt'l Bit out, mortified.

Rhonda is getting ready to go in, and she says, "Well, he certainly can run."

Becky is beaming at me.

"I hope you didn't video that for my mom," I say, dejected.

"You have no idea, do you?"

"Yeah. I got disqualified."

"Fifteen point two seconds. Calgary Stampede times."

"He knocked over every barrel."

I see Dunn, then moving toward us. He takes the bridle and looks up at me.

"You did real good, Kate," he says. "Cut yourself some slack. You're learning something new."

Becky is already planning the next gymkhana. "His potential is amazing," she says with enthusiasm. "If you can just control his excitement, he'll do great. I think if you had loped the outer track like they did—" She swings her head toward the two quarter horse girls.

Rhonda is just coming out of the arena. Her time is 18.3, which will win the barrels today.

I take Lt'l Bit for a slow lope around the outer track to calm him down, but the truth is, he is calm now. I am back in time to take him into the arena for my turn at the pole bending.

It is the same thing as soon as he goes through the gate. He is all charged up, snorting fire, and prancing, lunging forward. It is all I can do to hold him. The horn rings and he explodes across the line.

But this time, I don't know if it's me or him that is different, but he is way more controlled. He dances in and out of those poles like a skier doing slalom. They bend over, he is so close, but none of them go down.

When the announcer calls our time, I am shocked. In all those dozens of practice runs in the pasture, this is the best time we've ever had, at 24.5 seconds. I am on pins and needles as the other girls do the poles, but no one can touch our time. Rhonda, on that big horse, isn't even close. I am in delirious. It is better than anything I ever dreamed of. My horse and I have just won first place in a pole-bending competition.

Lacey rides over and congratulates me, and there is not a hint of resentment in her tone. Rhonda ignores me, though.

Lt'l Bit has totally settled down for the obstacle course, which is good because the girl who rides after Lacey gets thrown when her horse takes exception to the steam coming from under the bridge they have to cross. Whoever built the course created the steam effect with dry ice, and it was supposed to look like mist rising off the water in the morning.

I am not sure I have ever felt so focused as I do when I ride into that arena. There are four obstacles and they have to be done in order. First is the gate, which we have some trouble with, because I have trouble getting Lt'l Bit in close enough for me to lean over and undo the latch. But he marches over the steaming bridge with aplomb, steps over a wall constructed of branches and twigs as if he has never been so bored, allows me to grab a halter off one fence post and move it to another and then we are done. He lopes back to the finish line, and when people start applauding, he gives a little kick with his hind end that makes everyone laugh. I think the obstacles might be my favorite event because I felt so focused and as if we were a team, not as if I was just holding on for dear life, a passenger along for the ride. I came in third in the obstacles.

We barely had enough people to do the relay; we had four people on one team, and three on the other, so one of us, which was me, had to ride twice. Honestly, even though my team did not win, it was so much fun, and everyone laughed so hard as we tried to get those eggs in spoons across the arena, and then transfer them to the next team member, without breaking them.

After all the categories were done for all the age groups, we all went and sat in a line in front of the announcers' stand, and they announced placements and gave out ribbons.

In my age category, I got the first place ribbon for pole-bending. I have never seen a ribbon so beautiful. Big and silky and blue, with first place written in the button in the middle in gold letters. I also got third place for the obstacles, which was a white ribbon, and the red second place ribbon in the relay, which was kind of funny, because there was only two teams.

The other riders were leaning forward, and attaching the ribbons to their horse's bridles, and I did that too. A reporter from the paper took our picture. And then, one by one, we broke out of the line, and loped around the arena one more time, while everybody cheered for us. It sounded like a thousand people, even if there were less than fifty spectators in the stands.

I think that may have been the happiest moment of my whole life.

You know what was really neat? Becky was as happy as I was, and she didn't even win anything.

We tied Lt'l Bit to her dad's trailer, and looked after him, and while we did that her dad went and bought us hotdogs. Then we went and sat in the empty bleachers and ate hotdogs and looked at the videos Becky had taken on my mom's phone. I could actually laugh at the one of my crazy excited horse knocking over every barrel. In the pole-bending one, I didn't look nearly as ready for the Calgary Stampede as I thought I was, but I couldn't wait to show the video to my mom, anyway. The only thing that stopped it from being perfect, was that my mom hadn't been there to see it. For some reason, ever since Grandma Lemon phoned, I don't feel as mad at my mom as I did when we first moved here.

Dunn came over, and Becky and her dad wandered away to get some cotton candy, but I stayed and I showed him the videos. You could tell he was a little startled to be watching videos on a phone. This is a man who says Jumping Jehoshaphat after all!

"This isn't his first rodeo," Dunn says, as he watches the video of Lt'l Bit getting all frenzied before the starting horn goes off.

"But how could they give him up? Whoever had him before me?"

"There's lots of reasons people give up a good horse. They can't afford him anymore, or they're moving to a place where they can't have one. Or they've outgrown him and want something better. Or they've just lost interest."

"But don't you know which of those it is? Where did you get him from?"

He hesitates. "I got him and Eclipse off the meat wagon. Sometimes I put them on, and sometimes I take them off."

"The meat wagon? He was being sent to the slaughter house?" I am stunned by this. "Who could do that to Lt'l Bit?"

Dunn lifts that shoulder. "Lots of people in these parts who have horses are pragmatic about it, not romantic. For some reason, for some one, he'd outlived his usefulness. A lucky day for you, because thousand-dollar horses that are any good are harder to come by than perogies at a pie-eating contest."

That almost makes me smile, despite what he is telling me. That someone, maybe a girl just like me, was so hard-hearted that she took this little horse who gave his all to everything he did, and put him on a truck that was going to the slaughter house.

It makes me wonder about love all over again. Didn't whoever had Lt'l Bit before me love him at all?

"Some people won't tolerate a horse that's hard to catch," Dunn says. "Plus, he's not young anymore. Maybe they thought it was the kindest thing. We'll never know."

We go back to watching the videos, and we are on the last one, of the egg and spoon race, when the phone started ringing. I answered it hoping it was my mom. But it wasn't. It was my dad.

Chapter 12

MY DAD

IT WAS OBVIOUS that my dad was as surprised to hear my voice as I was to hear his. After a shocked silence, he said, *hello, sugarplum.*

Then, before I even say hello, he says Grandma told him this was Mom's number. It's kind of a relief to know my mother does not have a secret life and has been talking to my dad without me knowing it.

"Is Mom there?" he says.

"No, I have her phone."

"Where are you guys? I miss you. I need to see you. My lawyer says I have a right to see you. I can explain everything."

It is his salesman's voice, confident and suave. I don't know why. I just hang up the phone without saying anything, and then I turn it off, and put it in my pocket.

Maybe I was being mean, and trying to hurt him as bad as he had hurt us.

But I think it was more that I knew perfect days are pretty hard to come by, and I wasn't going to let him wreck it.

Though it was pretty much wrecked anyway. *I. I. I. I* miss. *I* need. *I* have rights. *I* can explain.

Nothing about *me*. How are you? Are you okay? I'm sorry my actions have resulted in your pain. Nothing like that.

"You look like you seen a ghost," Dunn says, and his eyebrows were furrowed up like he was worried. "You okay?"

"Yes," I say, but I am shaking my head *no* at the same time.

"Who was that?" Dunn says, and he sounds like he would reach through the phone and grab them by the neck and give them a good shake if he could.

I look around to see if anyone is listening, but Dunn and I are alone on the bleachers. "It was my dad."

Dunn doesn't say anything, so I just keep talking.

"Do you remember I asked you if you knew what a Chester Catcher was?"

"Yeah, I remember."

"There's this guy, in Vancouver. He calls himself the Chester-the-Molester Catcher. He goes online and he pretends he's a fourteen-year-old girl. He starts going back and forth with guys. Older guys. Way older guys. They do disgusting things like send him pictures of their privates. When they think he is a little girl. But then the Chester-the-Molester Catcher sets a trap. He arranges to meet them.

"And he gets the meeting recorded on a phone, just like Becky just did with gymkhana. These old men thinking they are meeting a young girl, and that she wants to... do things with them."

Dunn says a really bad swear word under his breath.

"Sometimes the Catcher posts it online. But sometimes he sends it to the news, because he doesn't have a real person's name, and he thinks someone might recognize who it is."

For a long time, I don't say anything. Dunn doesn't say anything either. He just waits.

"That's what happened to my dad," I finally say.

"The news showed it. With his face blocked out. But someone recognized his tie."

My dad knew he'd been caught. The night after Janey came up to me in school, he tells my mom he has something to tell her.

He says that this young girl started chatting to him online, and she was really screwed up, and he was worried she was going to get in over her head acting like that online, so he decided to meet her and have a chat with her, to protect her really, from herself.

My mom actually believes him, and thinks he is some kind of hero. Until the cops show up at our condo and seize all the computers. I am there when it happens, and my mom is crying, and telling one of the cops what *really* happened.

The cop flips open his phone, and finds a picture on it, and shows it to my mom.

"What part of that," he says with disgust, "has anything to do with helping a poor, screwed-up little girl stay out of trouble?"

It is a picture my dad emailed the Chester Catcher, when he thought he was emailing a fourteen-year-old girl. I don't know exactly what the picture is, but I can, unfortunately, guess.

I hear my mom screaming at him that night. "One year older than Katie! One year! What is wrong with you?"

My dad, who has an answer for everything, doesn't have an answer for that. He leaves and slams the door behind him as if my mom is being unreasonable. And unfair. As if he is the victim of all this.

There is nothing on the home computers, but then they go to my dad's office, and his computer there has all kinds of stuff on it, including all his interactions with the Chester Catcher. My mom tries to protect me, but

I hear her on the phone with Granny Wilson, sobbing, and saying, "He lured them with a picture of himself from when he was in high school."

The police come and get me, and take me to an office where there is a social worker, who asks me all these questions, but the truth is my dad never did anything to me.

Except if I'm really honest?

There was something on his face the day I tried on those jodhpurs, that made me feel really uncomfortable, almost sick to my stomach.

But that's all. And I've never breathed a word of that to anyone. I am certainly not going to tell Dunn McLeod that now.

I draw in a deep breath. My hands are shaking. "Now he says he has a right to see me," I tell Dunn.

Dunn squints off into the distance, and when he looks back at me, I wonder how I ever thought he was ugly.

He says, "Katie, you are the one with the rights, now. He lost his. And that doesn't mean you will never see him again, but when and if you do, you'll be the one to decide that. You and your mom."

"Do you think I should? See him?" I am a bit shocked that he sees it as an option at all. No one else—except maybe my Grandma and Grandpa Lemon—does.

"I can't tell you that. But I can tell you this. I've been on this planet a long time. And I've learned a thing or two, most of it from horses. And this is what horses have taught me: there is a bit of good in the worst of them; and a bit of bad in the best of them. As far as I can see people are exactly the same."

Since I was kind of expecting Dunn to say he would shoot my dad if he ever laid eyes on him, or be like the police and ask what else had happened, that was the most surprising answer of all.

Ever since it happened, I've only been able to think of my dad's faults: how he manipulates his clients to buy more expensive houses then they want; how he says cruel and nasty things about people; how sometimes he drinks too much; how he spends way too much money and plays the bigshot.

I think I do that so that it won't hurt so much that he isn't in my life anymore. But the truth is, it hurts anyway.

When Dunn reminds me there is good in everyone, I think about some of my dad's good things.

I think of how funny he was, and how generous, and how his face lit up when my mom and I gave him that stupid tie with Eeyore on it. I think of how he stayed up all night in the chair next to my bed when I got the sick because some dumb girl in our school hadn't got her vaccinations. I think of him swimming right beside me, out to the float at the cottage when I was seven, and how knowing he was there gave me the courage to do it. I think of him naming the constellations above our heads as the sparks from the fire flew toward them and the sticky marshmallow hardened on my fingers.

I realize I am, after all, half of him. I hope it is the good half.

When I speak though, my voice is small, like the voice of a little girl.

"He had everything. He had the most beautiful home, and he was the best at his job." I am trying not to cry. "He had us. He had me and my mom."

I think of all the love I thought we had. "How could we not be enough?" I whisper.

Dunn is quiet for the longest time. "Some men have

to lose everything to find out what enough is," Dunn says. "And for other men, there is never enough."

I'm pretty sure I know which of those men my dad is, and which one Dunn is, too.

"Do you miss them?" I ask him.

He doesn't ask who I mean or how I know.

He blinks hard, and his voice is a growl. "Oh, yeah."

And then, maybe because of what I just told him about us, he starts talking.

"I have a dream sometimes. I wake up right after I had it. My little girl was ten when she died, but in the dream, she is always three. She's riding Benny, a little Shetland pony I got for her. Her head is thrown back and she is laughing, and Grace is on the other side of her, looking at me with a look that is so pure..." his voice dies away and then he gathers himself.

"I wonder if I dream of that, because that was the time I had it. I had enough. And I never recognized it until it was too late.

"But sometimes, after I have that dream? It feels like a promise. That maybe it will be that way again, just for a little moment here or there. I hang onto that, on the bad days."

I recognize I have been given the rarest of gifts— Dunn McLeod gives me a little piece of his heart.

He clears his throat then, and seems embarrassed, a man of few words, who thinks he has said too much.

"When—if—you see your dad, you'll set the terms, not him," Dunn says. "A meal in a restaurant, a hot chocolate in a coffee shop."

Out of the corner of my eye, I see Becky coming, with two cones of candy floss so big you can't see her face at all, just the purple pom-pom on top of her "coach" toque.

I had a whole list of things beyond hotdogs that my lips never touched when my dad was part of my life: hot chocolate being among them. And also potato chips, Cheezies, doughnuts and soda pop. I suddenly can't wait to eat candy floss because Dunn is right: it's on my terms now.

I thought, maybe if I told someone else what had happened with my dad, I would feel sick with shame after, as if I had betrayed my own family.

But that's not how I feel, at all. I feel lighter, as though I have been carrying a weight around, and it has finally been lifted. And this is what I was not expecting: to feel so free about not needing my dad's approval anymore.

I like what Dunn said about me having the power now, especially today when I won my first blue ribbon.

I came first, even though when I first looked at those girls on their shiny, muscled-up thirty-thousand-dollar horses, it seemed as if that was going to be impossible.

I turn to Dunn, just as Becky starts to make her way up the bleachers, and I throw my arms around him and I hug him hard. For saving my horse. But more, for being worthy of the fragile trust I have bestowed on him, whether he wants it or not. I never want to let him go, but he puts me gently and firmly away from him, and I can't tell you how much I love it that Dunn absolutely hates me hugging him.

Chapter 13

HAPPINESS

I SENT THE video of the barrel race to my own email, so I could study it later and see how to fix things. Then I erased it off my mom's phone so she wouldn't see it. She had enough to worry about now that my dad had called, though as far as I know, he didn't call back. If he did, she didn't tell me. She watched all the pole-bending, and the obstacle course, and the relay race, over and over again, as if she couldn't believe what she was seeing.

Which, I'm going to guess, was my happiness.

There are pictures in the paper the next week, and the gymkhana results are posted there as well. I'm referred to as "newcomer, Katie Wilson," but then they spell my name three different ways in the article: Katie Wilson; Katy Wilson and Katy Winslow; which Becky says is normal for the Um Yuck Times. They spell out Lt'l Bit's name, so he is Little Bit, and I think now that his name has been in the newspaper, it's kind of official.

Kids I don't even know are high-fiving me in the hallway for beating the P.V. girls, which is what they call people from Pleasant Valley.

Speaking of PV people, that girl, Lacey, found my last name because of the newspaper article, but she couldn't find me in the phonebook, so she called Becky and Becky told me we had been invited to the big Pleasant Valley gymkhana on Canada Day.

I like how Becky says *we*, because we really are a team, me and her and Lt'l Bit.

That feels as if it a long way away, school will be out for the summer. I am already worried how I would get there, but Becky says she will ask her dad. I am not sure how I feel about that. I don't want to be a mooch, and I am not sure how to offer to pay him.

Becky comes over twice that week after school and we practice the barrels. Without the crowd and the speaker system and the other horses, there is no getting Lt'l Bit worked up, and we don't see anything close to the times he did at the gymkhana.

Once he is going so fast, he loses his footing and falls down, which scares all three of us. I fly over his head and do a somersault, and he somersaults right beside me. We are both shaking—trembling like leaves—after, but unhurt. Becky makes me get right back on.

"You aren't a real horse person until you've taken a few tumbles," she tells me.

And she was right to make me get back on, because in a few minutes, both Lt'l Bit and I have our confidence back. I decide I am *never* telling my mom about it.

It probably doesn't matter anyway, because Becky's dad has to go to a cattle show on the Canada Day weekend, so he can't drive us over there.

"You should ask Dunn," Becky says.

I think of all Dunn has done for me all ready, and I am not sure if I can ask one more thing of him.

I think maybe Becky's dad felt bad that he couldn't trailer us to the Canada Day gymkhana, because he offers to borrow a horse for Becky from his niece, Becky's cousin, and drop it at my place for the weekend so that Becky and I can go riding.

Becky says there are hundreds of acres of riding trails close to my house, but I don't trust myself to find my way around them on my own.

So Becky arrives on Saturday morning at about ten and her dad unloads a horse from his trailer.

It is a gigantic thing, dapple grey with big feathers around its feet. It must be part draft horse. Lt'l Bit is quite anxious to meet the new horse, so for once, he is easy to catch.

They sniff noses and that doesn't go very well—the other horse makes a high-pitched squealing noise I've never heard before—so we tie them far apart to get ready.

We brush our horses and clean their feet, and saddle and bridle them. I've never done this before, but Becky shows me how to slip the bridle over the halter, and wrap the lead shank around the saddle horn so that we can tie the horses up for our picnic.

My mom has made us a lunch, complete with homemade cookies, which she is getting pretty good at making. She puts lots of chocolate chips in them because I've told her Becky has a bit of a weakness for chocolate.

My mom brings out our lunch in a brand-new horn bag that is a surprise for me. I can slip it right over my saddle horn. It has two pouches that go on either side of the horn, one holds sandwiches and cookies in one side, and there are two bottles of water in the other.

When we are ready to go, we both mount up, and Mom takes lots of pictures on her phone. I think we probably look like a circus act, with Becky on that great big horse and me on my little one.

Her big horse's name is Ethel, and it scares me a bit.

She tosses her head, and won't stand still. She keeps moving sideways, crossing her feet over each other.

"Mares," Becky says, with a roll of her eyes. You can tell from the way Becky sits on that horse, kind of slouched and relaxed, that she hasn't had a formal lesson in her whole life, but has been riding horses since before she could walk. Ethel shifts sideways, and Becky gives it a firm smack on the neck, not even bothered a little bit.

And speaking of Lt'l Bit, he seems quite annoyed with the big horse's poor behavior. At first opportunity he reaches over and bites her, and not a little nibble either, but a great chomp of shoulder flesh, and holding it in his teeth long enough that Ethel squeals her protest.

"I think you should change his name to Little Bite," Becky's dad says, and we all laugh, and then Becky and I are on our way out the lane, with my mom taking video on her phone.

Having established he will be the boss, Lt'l Bit gets out in front and walks fast. The big horse soon forgets to act up and is huffing and puffing trying to keep up.

We ride along the country road for a while, and then turn onto another one, and then turn again. It is a cloudless day, and the sun is beating down.

The last road has a dead end sign on it, and some barricades at the end of it, but Becky tells me just to get Lt'l Bit to step over the barricade. There is a well-worn trail right on the other side.

We follow it for maybe ten minutes, across a side hill, and then we are in the woods. I am still not used to how hot it gets in Um Yuck, and so going into the coolness of the woods is amazing, like stepping out of the sun into air conditioning. The forest smells good, and the light filters through the towering cedar and pine trees and dapples the trail in shadows of light and dark.

Becky is talkative, and she tells me she has a bit of a crush on Cam Wellington. She has to explain who he is, because I have no idea.

"This is the first time I've been in school with boys," I admit to her. I don't admit to her that it scares me a little.

She is astonished at the concept of an all-girls school and has lots of questions to ask about it.

I tell her of course we still had crushes on boys, but usually in a totally unrealistic way, like having a Justin Bieber poster taped to the inside of your locker. She finds that hilarious, and suddenly I do, too.

"Justin Bieber is so yesterday," I say, and she agrees, totally, and we talk about who we like today.

The trail forks, and Becky tells me to take the lower one, and we come to a place that is flat and wide open, and she says, "Let's go for a run."

And suddenly, my life is just like everything I ever imagined, only better. My friend and I are cantering our horses down a gorgeous wooded trail, and it is like a scene out of a movie, only so much better.

At the end of the running spot her horse is really huffing and puffing, and so is Lt'l Bit. There is a creek we have to cross. Lt'l Bit just marches through it, splashing happily, like there is nothing to it, but her horse sidles back and forth, snorting and rolling its eyes until I can see the whites of them.

No matter what she does, stupid Ethel won't cross the creek.

"Just keep going," Becky says. "I bet she's more scared to be by herself than she is to cross the water."

So I keep going down the trail and after about two

minutes, I hear Ethel whinny hysterically, and then I hear her crash through the water and come thundering down the trail behind me. I would be terrified, if I was Becky, but Becky seems to find it hilarious.

We take a fork in the trail to the left, and it winds up and up and up, through trees and small meadows, and past rock faces. At the top we come into a beautiful huge meadow, with wildflowers threaded through the grass. The flowers have yellow petals with little brown faces, like mini-sunflowers, and they are in bloom everywhere. I wish I would have brought my camera.

Even Lt'l Bit is really huffing and puffing now, so we decide this would be a great place to have a break. We tie up the horses, and loosen their cinches, and sit in the grass and have lunch. We can see all the way to Um Yuck.

Lt'l Bit shows his first bad behavior. He paws and whinnies. I'm pretty sure he is mad that I am eating lunch and he is tied up with all this grass around him.

So, I go untie him, and hold his lead shank loosely in my hand while we finish lunch. Becky adores my mom's chocolate chip cookies and Lt'l Bit adores the grass. Ethel, still tied up, is sulking and looking at us sideways.

For a few seconds, I debate whether to tell Becky about my dad, but then it seems as if it would just be wrong to spoil all this happiness, so, instead, I tell her how my mom is going to start teaching a yoga class two nights a week at the Rec Plex.

"I don't know if this town is ready for yoga," Becky says. "There are people who are still up in arms because the grocery store is open on Sunday."

I don't get the connection. I give Becky the last cookie, and after lunch, we explore some more trails.

A LITTLE BIT OF HEAVEN

Becky shows me how, with the big hill in the center of the trails, it is impossible to get lost.

By the time we head home it is really hot, and the last part of the ride is all out in the open. We get into the yard and unsaddle the horses, who are both soaked in sweat. Becky finds the hose that we use to fill the water trough, and she sprays her horse off. And then she hands me the hose and I run it over Lt'l Bit. We let them both go in the pasture, and watch them roll around. When they get up, Lt'l Bit lays his ears flat against his head, and lunges at Ethel who moves out of his way.

"He's just establishing the pecking order," Becky tells me.

It's quite funny that my little horse is determined to be the boss over the big galoot, but I think he has proven he is smarter than her. Way.

While I'm watching the horses, Becky sneaks up behind me with the hose and holds it over my head. The cold water is shocking and wonderful.

I run from her, squealing, and when I am so soaked it doesn't matter anymore, I go and wrestle the hose away from her, and put my thumb over the spout, just like she did. Our apartment in Vancouver did not lend itself to water fights, and so this is a first for me.

Pretty soon we are both wet through and screaming with laughter.

Out of the corner of my eye, I see my mom, standing in the shadow of the porch, watching us. I can see she is wearing one of her sundresses, but her face is in the shadows.

But I am willing to guess that worried furrow, that is in her forehead most of the time now, is gone and that she is smiling.

Chapter 14

HOME

I GET OFF the bus at Dunn's after school on Monday. I have to wander around a bit to find him, but I finally do. Beyond some trees behind his house, is a big riding arena, almost the same size as the one the gymkhana was on at the fairgrounds.

I stop in the shade of the trees and watch him. He is riding Eclipse and I am so aware that I could be around horses for the next fifty years and still not even be close to knowing all there is to know. Because Dunn is in a different league, totally, than anyone I have ever seen ride before, even on television.

Dunn carries a quietness inside of him. It burns kind of slow and warm, like a candle burning in a window on a stormy winter night. And that warmth is melting out of him and down into that horse.

Eclipse's head is low and relaxed. Her canter is a glorious thing, as if she is floating two feet off the ground, her hooves never touching. Dunn is not riding her, so much as a part of her. There seems to be no effort. I cannot discern commands from him to her at all.

As I watch that horse goes from flying down the arena at a full gallop and then stops so fast the sand is flying and she nearly sits down on her back legs. She pivots, and lopes the other way, slides to that stop again.

Then she is spinning in a tight circle around her own back legs, spinning so fast that it is a wonder either her or Dunn does not collapse from dizziness.

It is ballet on horseback.

Dunn suddenly seems to realize I am there. He brings it down to a walk—relaxed, an old cow poke riding drag on a herd—and comes over to the fence.

"Howdy," he says.

I start to grin. I can't help it. Who on earth says howdy in this day and age?

But I try it, too. "Howdy," I say and then I am giggling so hard my eyes start watering.

When I finally look back at him, he is smiling. You know what? He *does* look like Sam Elliot.

I hope he'll ask me if I want to ride Eclipse, but he doesn't.

"What can I do you for?"

"How come you don't do that anymore? Reining?"

He lifts that skinny shoulder, a gesture that is totally his own, and the hint of a smile is gone. "Lost interest, I guess. If you choose the right horse, and do it right, with lots of training and conditioning, it's not hard on the animal. But lots of people ride those horses too hard, doing nothing but spins and stops, until they got a horse so stove-up it can barely move. It's a hell of a price to pay to pander to ego."

"Did you rip down the sign on the outside of town?"

"People are still talking about that?" he says, not really answering, but it is an answer, nonetheless.

"Why?"

For a moment he looks irritated, but then he shrugs again. "Because I wasted precious time chasing something that wasn't worth the trade. What can I do for you?" he asks again.

"There's a gymkhana in Pleasant Valley on Canada Day."

He nods, like he knew that all ready.

"I've been invited to be in it. But I don't know how to get there."

I guess I was hoping he would volunteer, but he doesn't say anything.

"Do you think I could do something around here to earn you hauling me and Lt'l Bit and Becky over there?"

His brow furrows in thought, and after a very long minute, or two, he says, "This is a small, gossipy town, Katie. I don't think I want to be hauling two young girls around."

His honesty takes me aback, and I feel so rejected and embarrassed I look at my feet so that he won't see the shame in my eyes. I am sorry I ever told him about my dad. If I hadn't, he probably wouldn't have even known that sometimes old men look at young girls in the wrong way.

"Look at me."

I do. I see that he knew, long before I said anything, that there are some really wicked things in the world. I see that old-fashioned decency is so deep in him that it runs through his blood.

"I'll tell you what, if your mom can drive you and Becky over to Pleasant Valley, I'll take Lt'l Bit there for you. And my nephew comes to help around the place on Thursdays, after school, so you can come do some chores when he's here."

"I trust you, Dunn," I tell him quietly.

"I know you do, Katie. I aim to be worthy of that."

"You already are."

He turns away from me and starts to put the horse through her paces. It's a long walk home and he hasn't offered me a ride. And now I know why.

On Thursday, I get off the bus at Dunn's place. And so does a boy from school. He realizes we are going the same way, and introduces himself.

"Mike McLeod," he says.

I've seen him around school, and I should have guessed, really. He has that same lanky, loose-limbed way about him, and the same brown eyes. It seems as if he carries the same quiet inside of him. He doesn't have the bloodhound look, though. He's probably two years older than me and kind of cute and it makes me feel as if I have nothing in the world to say.

But I manage to choke out, "So, you work for your uncle?"

"Yeah. I break green colts for him."

"Green?" I ask astonished.

His smile is slow, just like Dunn's. And he says, "Not Kermit the Frog green. Young horses that haven't been ridden. Uncle Dunn does the groundwork, and I put the first ride on them."

I don't have a clue what groundwork is, but I think it is probably what he was doing with Eclipse that time I saw him standing in the round pen with her.

"Uncle Dunn's says he's getting too old to get tossed off horses," Mike volunteers.

"He *is* old," I say, and we both have a little chuckle over that.

My job, it turns out, involves poop. In fact, my life, these days seems to have a lot to do with poop. I have to pick up Lt'l Bit's "lotsa" bits, and that's my job at Dunn's, too. I get a wheelbarrow, just like the one at home, and a shovel, and I go out in the pens and shovel nuggets into the wheelbarrow and then bring them to a big pile.

You'd think all that poop wouldn't be much fun, but

let me tell you, dealing in horse poop is not the same as dealing in something really revolting, like dog poop. I kind of like being outside, and being around the horses, and watching Mike McLeod out of the corner of my eye. He is just like his uncle when he is on a horse, radiating quiet and calm and confidence. He is pretty focused, so I don't think he even notices me.

My mom comes and gets me, on her way home from work, so I don't have to walk home.

Mike sees me at school the next day. I am with Becky and Marcie and I know he could ignore me altogether or say something mean, like how I pick up poop and he rides horses, but he doesn't. He just lifts his hand a bit and says, *Hi Katie.* He doesn't smile or make a big deal out of it, but somehow I feel *seen.* I can tell Mike McLeod really is like his uncle in a lot of ways.

Marcie says *ooo-la-la* under her breath, but neither of them asks how I know him. The truth is most people in Um Yuck know each other, and I'd say ninety per cent of the kids at school are bumping into their relatives in the hallways and on Main Street.

That weekend, Becky's dad takes Becky and his nurse girlfriend to Calgary for some shopping and a show. Becky is excited to go, so I guess it is not as a bad a betrayal to her mom as a week in Puerto Vallarta would have been.

My mom has been asked to work an extra shift because someone is sick, so I wake up to a quiet house and no agenda which is new, after my highly scheduled life in Vancouver. I have kept pretty busy here, too, so I kind of like this lazy nothing-to-do feeling. I lay around in bed, but after a while it gets old, so I decide to go for a ride by myself.

I am a little nervous at first, mostly about finding the

trails again without Becky's help. But Lt'l Bit is calm and even easy to catch, and finding the trails is a cinch.

One thing I am aware of, that I was not so aware of when I did this with Becky, is the sound once I enter the woods. There is sound and plenty of it: birds calling and leaves whispering against each other. Sometimes the trees even creak, like an old door opening.

Lt'l Bit's feet make a steady clip-clop on the ground, but it, like everything else, seems muffled. The beauty—all the shades of green and the way the light comes through the trees—is unearthly. I am also aware I have never been quite this alone before. There is no one around. And no one even knows where I am. I grew up with the constant brushing of shoulders with my fellow man, so maybe that is why I find this solitude almost incomprehensible and weirdly exhilarating.

We follow the same trail we took before, Lt'l Bit knows it now. He even breaks into a canter at the same spots. I don't think there is any chance of getting lost.

He is huffing and puffing by the time we get to the top where the meadow is, so I decide to take a break. I get off and loosen his saddle, and I get my lunch out of the horn bag.

I sit down in the meadow and juggle my sandwich and his lead rope, so that both of us can eat. The brown-eyed Susans are nearly done, but the meadow is threaded through with new wildflowers. I don't have any idea what they are called, and it doesn't really matter. There are yellow ones, and bright blue ones, purple ones, and red ones.

From up here, I can see almost all the way to Um Yuck. A big bird is floating on the air currents above me, and I see it is a bald eagle. It circles higher and higher until I can't see it anymore.

I don't know if I've ever felt this way before. Maybe, kind of, on the first night that Lt'l Bit came home. I feel the way Dunn looks when he rides a horse: as if I have melted into everything, as if I am not separate from it, but a part of it. I feel this quiet glory within me, that I don't think has a name, but it is sacred and silent and it makes me feel as if I am full to the top.

After I finish eating some crackers and cheese, I lie down in the tall meadow grass and look up at the sky. I realize how perfect Lt'l Bit's name is, after all.

Because, really? Don't we experience heaven in little bits? In glimpses and in moments? I see the eagle again, circling, and the clouds floating against an endless sea of azure blue. I hear the buzz of life all around me, and it doesn't disgust me like it did just a few weeks ago. I can smell the sweetness of the grass that is crushed below me, and an earthy smell that I can't identify.

My eyes close and I savor this moment, this little bit of heaven.

When I startle awake, at first I don't know where I am. Then I remember and sit up, my heart pounding when I realize I don't have the lead rope anymore.

But Lt'l Bit is still there, grazing at the edge of the meadow, watching me out of the corner of his eye.

I pick up my horn bag and I get up and walk toward him, but he sidles away. He coughs a couple of times. I go through the horn bag and find an apple, but for once in his life he is not interested.

Now that I am awake, he decides it is time to go home, and he finds the trail, and walks down it, just a few steps ahead of me. If I quicken my pace in hopes of catching him, he just quickens his, too.

He does not even show mercy when it is time to cross the creek. He splashes across it, and waits for me on the other side, nibbling a branch. I take off my boots and wade in, and its then I realize that I'm not even angry, that nothing seems to be able to erase that feeling I had in the meadow before I went to sleep. The water feels deliciously cool on such a warm day, and the mud squishes up between my toes. I dry off my feet as best I can and shove them back in my socks. As soon as I get my boots back on, he is off again.

Once we are out of the forest, he gets quite a bit ahead of me, walking fast, breaking into a trot sometimes, until finally I lose sight of him altogether. He appears to be a horse on a mission, though I don't know what that would be. I run as much as I can, because I am scared my mom will be home and that the horse coming into our yard without me on it will give her a heart attack.

But when I get there, her van is still gone, and Lt'l Bit is waiting for me at the pasture gate, eager to get in, not the least contrite for making me walk all that way.

His mission was to get home, and it is obvious he is happy to have accomplished it.

In Vancouver, my mom had a friend who she met through her yoga class, who was a biologist. Dr. Ames and my mother used to sometimes sit and sip expensive wine all afternoon, and I remember her saying once, her voice shrill and insistent, that animals did not have feelings, that they were not *sentient.*

I had to look it up in the dictionary, and basically to be sentient means to be aware or conscious, to be able to perceive or feel things. I wish Dr. Ames could see my little horse right now. Nobody could look at him and not know how full of mischief he is, and how pleased he is with himself!

I open the gate and let him in, and *now* he stands

still while I get the tack off of him. The saddle is so loose I am surprised it didn't slip sideways when he walked home. I brush him and tell him this is kind of thing is probably *exactly* why he got put on the meat wagon, but I say it without any heat at all. As soon as I slip the halter off, he goes and lies on the ground and rolls around in a great cloud of dust. He snorts his pleasure as he gets up and shakes himself off. Just like with Dunn, it seems absurd that I once found him ugly. It occurs to me Dunn and Lt'l Bit have not changed at all, so that the change must be in me.

Right now, it actually feels as if my heart could burst for loving my little horse, even though he can be so bad.

I guess that's how my mom feels about me, even when I am being so mean to her.

I look around and realize this *is* home now. Not so much the house and the pasture, but the way I feel inside. At ease in my new life. Comfortable.

And as if I am closer, somehow, to being me than I ever have been before. Maybe that is what home is, after all, the one place in the world where it is absolutely safe to be yourself.

Chapter 15

HEART

THE PLEASANT VALLEY Gymkhana is quite a bit bigger than the Um Yuck one was. There are probably fifty contestants in all the categories, and there is a covered grandstand, not just bleachers, which seems to be full of people.

There is lots of noise and commotion, and some of the horses seem quite jittery about it, including Lacey's big quarter horse.

Lt'l Bit is not in the least perturbed. As I get him ready, he yawns and gives his braided main a shake, as if to say *ho-hum*.

There are two arenas here, one for warming up and one for the actual events, so I take him to the warm up one, and Becky, wearing her crazy toque, though it is probably going to be ninety degrees today, coaches us through some slow canters and figure eights. I have Lt'l Bit back up and move off my leg to the right and the left.

I can hear the announcer in the background as I warm up. He sounds like an old cowboy, and he is quite funny. He says things like "And now we have the little folk on their dwarf horses. Ain't that the cutest thing you ever seed? Oh, we have our first buck off of the day and poor Alfie Connell is havin' hisself a dirt sandwich."

My age category has eleven contestants in it. Becky

is vibrating with nervousness. I am going to ride seventh in all three events, which she says is really good, because you don't want to be first or last. We line up on the other side of the fence, ready to go in. I scan the stands, and see my mom and Dunn sitting together. My mom waves at me.

My turn comes, and in the background I can hear the announcer, saying, "Now what we got here, folks? Looks like a little backward Appaloosa. Them spots is in all the wrong places..."

But I am so intensely focused it is as if his voice is muffled, the way it would be if I was riding in the deepest forest.

Lt'l Bit is charged up, but not as bad as he was last time. The warm up has helped. The horn blares and he explodes forward. We touch the first barrel, but it does not go over, and I am already have my head cranked, looking to the second one. I can feel it: that melting together, that exact moment when our energy joins, and we are one power, surging forward. We come around the third barrel, and I don't even have to prod him. He flattens out for the finish line, and just as he crossed, he kicks up his back legs, way over his head. I nearly come off of him, but somehow I don't. The crowd goes wild for him.

We are both breathless when we come to a halt. Becky is jumping up and down. I can hear the announcer in the background, saying "Ooo-eee, ladies and gents, what we have here is a little stick of dynamite." Our time is an astounding 15 flat with no penalties.

I glance at my mom. She doesn't look happy. She looks petrified. And it looks as if Mike McLeod is sitting there, too. I decide I'm not looking at the stands anymore.

I am in a trance watching the rest of the riders go, holding my breath, hoping against hope: and then there it is. All the riders have finished, and no one has touched my time.

Becky is screaming, and we high five, and then I have to keep focused for the poles. Two of the contestants before me have time penalties for knocking poles down. Lacey posts a really good time.

And then it is my turn.

"Ladies and gents, here they are, Miss Katie, riding Stick-o-Dynamite."

The horn goes off, and again, Lt'l Bit leaps into it, dodging in and out of those poles, his whole body bending around them, serpentine. He flattens out to race back to the finish line, and again, just as he crosses, he kicks up. The crowd loves him. And he seems to love the crowd. Not sentient? Ha.

Again, we post the best time so far, and again, the announcer editorializes a bit, "Ladies and gents, what we got here is a little bit of a horse with a whole lot of heart."

No one can touch our time.

The obstacles are crazy. Someone has come up with the bright idea of putting a chicken in a cage, and you have to pick up the cage from one spot and carry it to the other.

Most of the horses take exception to this being asked of them, and by the time it is my turn three of them have been disqualified, and one rider has "had herself a dirt sandwich." I'm glad it wasn't Lacey, who got through the course but looks pale and shaky riding out of the arena, her horse all lathered up and showing the whites of his eyes.

Lt'l Bit saunters through first obstacle, the gate,

which I have practiced endlessly. He crosses the bridge with a yawn, and then we come to the chicken, who isn't really enjoying this any more than the horses. It sees me coming and starts squawking and flapping its wings.

Little Bit stops beside it, and I lean over to pick up the cage. He shows the chicken his big yellow teeth, and takes a little nip at the cage as if the chicken is irritating him enormously. The crowd roars their approval as I pick up the cage and move it from one station to the other. We do the last obstacle and exit the arena to deafening applause. I even glance at my mom. She is standing up and clapping. Mike McLeod gives me a thumbs-up.

I post the best time for the obstacles as well.

The relay is next and we have four teams. This time we all have to take off our boots at one end and leave them down there, then ride in our socks back to the finish line. Your team has to gallop down, one person at a time, get a pair of boots on, and ride back, tag the next member who rides down. The thing is, you don't have to put on your own boots, just shove on the closest ones, so in the end one poor girl is standing there with a tiny pair of boots she doesn't have a hope of squeezing onto her feet.

It is more for fun than for prizes and it is so much fun, and the laughter from both the crowd and the participants makes such a good release from the tension of competition. My team comes in second and Lacey's comes in first and I'm genuinely happy for her.

We line up for our ribbons, and I have three first place ribbons and one second snapped on my bridle.

And then, they have one extra category here: it's called the grand aggregate, and it goes to the person who has accumulated the most points over the day: 4 points for each first place ribbon, three for each second place and so on.

And out of everybody there, even the adults, I win that, too.

And so I get to lead the final canter around the arena. I go around once by myself, and as I go around the announcer says, "Ladies and gents, us old cowboys have a word we reserve for that man, or that beast, that has that extra bit of try in them.

"That word is heart, and you are looking at a horse with a whole lot of that. Let's let him know we see it."

The crowd claps as though they will never stop. And we are cantering around, and Lt'l Bit is kicking up his heels, in all his glory.

We come out of the arena, and I see Becky, so excited she is crying. I ride toward her, planning to give her half of those ribbons, when I feel him stumble.

And then he staggers sideways.

Somehow I throw myself clear as Lt'l Bit's legs collapse underneath him, and he hits the ground so hard it shakes, as if a giant has fallen.

Chapter 16

TIME

L T'L BIT SCRAMBLES to his feet again, almost as if he's embarrassed by what happened.

"Did you trip on something?" Becky asks.

We both search the ground, even though other riders are coming out, looking for a slippery spot or a hole, but there doesn't seem to be anything.

Dunn and my mom arrive, breathless, and I know from my mom's face she has seen what happened.

"You could have been killed," she says.

Dunn just looks grim.

He goes around Lt'l Bit, putting his hands on his legs and his stomach. He even bends over and puts his ear to his chest.

"Has he fallen before?" he asks.

"Once. But I think he just lost his footing coming around a barrel."

My mom is glaring at me as if I have kept State's secrets from her.

"Anything else?"

I shake my head. "A little cough every now and then."

"Okay. Let's load him up and get him home. I think we better have a vet look at him."

My mother blanches slightly. What is that going to cost on a holiday?

Three hours later we are all at my place, and the vet

has her stethoscope to Lt'l Bit's chest. "There's definite arrhythmia," she says.

I've never really been one of those people who thinks about what I want to be when I grow up, but despite the fact I am sick with worry about Lt'l Bit, somehow when I see Dr. Johannsen, and how confident she is despite the fact she is tiny, I think *that's it. That's what I'm going to be some day.*

Dr. Johannsen straightens and lets her stethoscope dangle and begins to knead Lt's Bit under his chin. Then her fingers stop, and her shoulders droop.

"Katie, I'm sorry. I think your horse may have myocardial disease. Dunn, I should have caught it when I vet checked him for you, but his heart probably doesn't do that all the time."

I am trying to figure out what *myocardial disease* is. I can tell from the look on her face she thinks it is something really bad.

Dr. Johannsen is kneading under Lt'l Bit's chin again. "This is what I missed. He's had strangles, I can feel the scar tissue where it erupted, here, under his chin. The hair has not come back completely, so it's probably recent. My guess is he's been overwhelmed by *Streptococcus equi.* His heart muscle has probably been inflamed for some time."

"It's probably why they shipped him in the first place," Dunn says. His face is taut.

"But we can fix it, right?" I ask. Becky comes and stands beside me. She takes my hand, which I take as a very bad thing. She's been around animals her whole life. She *knows.*

No one will look at me. The vet starts packing up her things.

"I'm sorry, sweetheart," she says. She pats me awkwardly on the shoulder, still not looking at me. "You'll know when it's time."

"Time for what?" I whisper. Becky squeezes my hand.

"You can't ride him," Dr. Johannsen says. "At all. He could collapse again."

The vet gives Dunn a sad look, and puts her things in the back seat of her truck.

"Time for what?" I say louder, to Dunn. If Becky squeezes my hand any harder she's going to break it.

Dunn slips the halter off Lt'l Bit, and we all watch as he walks off into the pasture and starts eating, watching us out of the corner of his eye.

I shake loose of Becky's grip on me, and turn to Dunn, and I am going to ask again, only the answer is written all over him.

Just like that, I know Dunn's flaw. Even in a cruel world, he has hope. He wants to save every one of those horse coming through his place, being shipped to the slaughter house. I doubt he sees the irony in the similarities of the names: McLeod and Macleod. One saves. One kills.

He wants it so bad that he tried to save a little horse that was already done, who, unbeknownst to Dunn or even the vet who checked him over, had such a big heart it was outgrowing his body.

Whoever put him on that trailer knew he was done. They knew he had outlived his usefulness. Maybe they thought, *well, why not make a few bucks off the poor guy?* Or maybe they thought it was the most humane way to end it for him.

No matter what their reason, it seems unbearably heartless, and it seems as if they missed precious moments like this one: a little horse, delicately nibbling grass, seeking out the tender new pieces. They missed him kicking up his heels, one last time, for the crowds. They missed him sucking on apples, and his delight in finding his way home.

My mom's friend would say he didn't *feel* anything, that it is ridiculous to assign human emotion to an animal. But watching him now, I can't help but wonder, does he know he got a reprieve? Or does he just live in that place, the one I have only entered twice, and both times because of him. That place where all there is this, the sacredness of a single breath.

Whoever put him on that trailer bound for death missed his moments. And I got them instead.

There is still a few precious hours or days or weeks left.

I have never looked at time like this before: a gift that runs out.

Dunn claps me on the shoulder. "Doc was right. You'll know when it's time. And when it is, you call me. Day or night. And I'll come look after it."

"How?" I whisper.

"He won't even know it's coming."

"You're going to shoot him," I say, and I hear a certain resolve in my voice. My mother, who has been silent, flinches. She turns away. I know she is crying.

"It's quick and it's painless," Becky reassures me quietly.

I nod. I feel grown up. And like I am worthy of this tremendous responsibility that has been passed to me.

To know when it is time.

Chapter 17

LIGHT

I KNOW I am not supposed to ride him, but in those long, hot days of summer, sometimes, if he wanders close to fence, I will clamber on his back, and wrap my legs around him. I lay down on him, my face buried in his mane, and my arms wrapped around his neck, trying to memorize the scent that comes off him.

I know Lt'l Bit so well now that I know that scent is strongest and sweetest at his wither. I run the coarse hair of his mane through my fingertips again and again, feel the fluid movement of his muscles underneath me as he moves from piece of grass to piece of grass.

I notice the sensitivity of him: he can feel a single fly land on his back and shake it off with a quiver of a muscle. I notice how his ears swivel toward the smallest sound, and prick straight forward when he is alert. I notice the inside of his nostrils flares bright pink.

I have put a sprinkler in the pasture to encourage a few blades of new grass to grow for him. He still can make me laugh. In the heat of the day, he will go put his head in the spray and close his eyes, and sigh with utter contentment as the water sluices down his face.

I finally have my horse that acts just like a movie horse. When I come out of the house, his head comes up, and he whinnies his excitement and lopes toward me.

But, these days, even the smallest lope across the pasture leaves him wheezing for breath. The cough has become persistent. He lies down more than he used to.

Of course, now, there is a reason for his devotion to me: it is all reward and no work for my little horse. I never come to him without my pockets bulging with apples or carrots, or horse cookies that I buy at the feed store with some of the money I make working for Dunn.

Now that school is out, I go almost every day. Becky can't believe I would rather shovel poop than hang out at the swimming hole underneath the bridge with her, but somehow that is what I want. Even on the hottest days.

And I still do shovel poop, but now he is having Mike, who works there all summer, show me how to do groundwork, too. I don't even feel self-conscious around Mike anymore. We are both so focused on what we are doing that we don't focus on each other.

Well, mostly. Now and then I do notice how thick and tangled his eyelashes are. Or that one of his front teeth kind of crosses over the other one. I notice, sometimes, the way the light spins the hair on his forearms to gold.

But mostly I just see the wonder of a horse, who was trembling with trepidation, come around. It's awesome when it is a young horse, who has never had any work done with it before.

But when it is one of those old horses that Dunn takes off the meat wagon, the ones that are so filled with fear that the sour smell of it is clinging to them? When it is one of those, who has reacted to you with pure terror, and trembles if it feels trapped and you approach it? If it is one of those who can't stand to have their heads touched, who sometimes have scars on them where someone has beat them, or where they've injured themselves with their own stupidity? When it is one of those who takes that tentative first step toward you, head down, cautiously curious? That is more than awesome. More than rewarding.

That is being in the Light.

Summer is almost over when time runs out.

In the end, my noble little horse made the decision for me. I went out in the first light to give him some hay and an apple, before I went to Dunn's, and the pasture was eerily empty. He had, I thought, almost hopefully, escaped.

I thought he had found one last piece of mischief in himself, and that he had opened the gate, and that I would find him down the road, happily chomping on Becky's aunt's begonias.

Only then I saw there was a little hill, a hump, where there had been none before, way in the back corner of the pasture.

I ran to it, but I stopped short of it, hoping to see a breath. But the pile was motionless.

He was gone. Really gone. There was nothing left of him in that mound of horse, the color of a dirty city snow drift, that lie on the ground. I stared at him. His spirit had flown completely.

I eased in a little closer. His eyes were glazed, and his teeth were exposed in a grimace. His mane lifted in the breeze and even that seemed unnatural. I fell to my knees, and then laid my whole body across his body. There was still faint warmth there. I rested my head against his sweet smelling wither one more time. I kissed him, and I took my fingers and closed his eyes. I stayed there until there was no warmth left.

In a daze I went to the house.

My mom was sipping coffee. It was her day off. She was still in her housecoat.

"Can you call Dunn?"

She looks at me, and the coffee mug freezes half way to her lips. In slow motion, she puts it down, and is getting up, coming toward me.

Her voice is like it is coming from underwater, agonizingly slow, "Oooohhhhh, Kateeeee."

I can't stand the thought of being touched, as if I will crumble like that glass windshields are made out of, into a million crumbly pieces of diamond. I run out the door. I can't go back out to that little mound that was, such a short time ago, a living, breathing being. Where did he go? How can such a fragile thing as one breath separate us, life from death?

I go and I hide in the shed, climbing up in clean-smelling hay. I cry until my shirt is wet from it.

After a while, I hear Dunn's truck rattle up and stop right outside the hayshed. He gets out of the truck, and my mom is on him.

"How could you?" she is shrieking. "How could you?"

I put my eye to a crack in the grey weathered boards of the shed, and my mom is still in her housecoat and she is pounding on his chest and screaming at him, "How could you do this to her?"

Dunn lets her pound on him for a while, and then he puts his arms around her and pulls her in tight to him. He's not hugging her so much as containing her, pinning her arms so she'll stop hitting him.

She is sobbing now. I don't think I have seen my mom cry, ever, not even when all the stuff happened with my dad.

But she is wailing, an animal howl of pain and fury. It isn't just about Lt'l Bit. It's about everything. Betrayal and change and fear of failure and an uncertain future. It is the first time I realize, really realize, that all these changes have been every bit as hard on my mom as on me. But while I took all my pain out on her, and she protected me from hers.

"How could you?" she sobs into Dunn's shirt. "You sold Katie a heartbreak."

For the longest time, he doesn't say anything at all, just holds her tight, until the wailing quiets to little sobs.

And then he says, "I dunno, Penny, I always feel like love gives more than it takes."

Her voice is muffled by his chest. She is making no effort to break free of him. She says, "Tell that to a woman who didn't waste fifteen years of her life on a very bad man."

"Waste?" he says. "Oh, mama bear, you got it all so wrong. You think it's about protecting her so she never gets hurt. But that ain't it. It's letting her know she'll get hurt and aplenty, too. And that she'll survive. That's how you get it. That's how you get *heart*.

"You didn't waste your time. You got that girl out of the deal. I've been watching her work horses, and she's got more heart than ten men put together. In the horse business, we'd say that was a good trade."

There is silence then. My eyeball is glued to that crack in the boards. My mom is crying so hard I think she would collapse if Dunn was not holding her up.

I think of him saying that, *she's got more heart than ten men put together,* and I know that is the kind of faith you have to live up to.

And so I leave the hayshed, and I go to them, and I kind of push in between them, and put my arms around her, too.

Dunn steps away, and my mom and I are clinging

to each other crying until we are both soaked in each other's tears.

We are crying for everything. For a good horse with a big heart, and a bad man with a small one. For love, in all its sorrow and all its glory.

I allow myself to feel it completely. The strength of my mother's love for me. It is surrounding me and protecting me, just like it has always done, even when I refused to see it.

Dunn is standing off to the side, looking uncomfortable. He won't leave, though, not until he is satisfied that we will be all right.

Chapter 18

DARK

DUNN CAME OVER with a backhoe, and dug a trench, slipped that little horse inside it and covered it back up. Then Becky and my mom and me gathered around that mound, and had a ceremony. We all remembered something good about Lt'l Bit, though in truth it was the bad things about him—like him farting when he ran away—that made us laugh, and cry, the hardest.

When we were done remembering things, I took every single ribbon he had ever won for me, and I put long nails through them, and I punched the nails down deep into that mound of earth that covered my horse, my Lt'l Bit.

And then darkness descended.

I didn't want to go to Dunn's anymore. Or leave the house. Without asking, my mom got the internet again, and Netflix. Sometimes I stayed in my pajamas all day and watched movie after movie. Sometimes I didn't wash my hair for so long my mom had to remind me. I couldn't think of a single thing to say to Becky when she phoned.

Sometimes, I would think, *I am almost through this*, only to find I wasn't. It was like a dark storm, coming, and dumping on me, and just when I thought it was over it would circle back and hit me again.

I was scared to go out, even to the grocery store, because I could start crying in the blink of an eye. I could not even guess what would set me off: a whiff of aftershave that reminded me of my dad, a scarf the color of Lt'l Bit's halter, two Muskoka chairs set up outside a store.

It wasn't all about Lt'l Bit. Probably most of it wasn't about Lt'l Bit. He had helped me postpone the inevitable.

Because really? I earned my right to grief. I am the girl who has lost everything. My dad, my grandparents, my friends, my home, my lifestyle, my school, and now my horse.

School starts again, and I go through the motions. I have to say Becky and Marcie and Angela are amazing. They ask nothing of me, and never give up on me. They make sure I eat lunch with them, I am always invited to movies and stuff, though I never go.

Sometimes, on a bad day, when I feel as if I just want to hide out in the washroom, they come and circle me, like warriors assigned to guard duty.

Mike will come out of his way to say hi to me, and to ask how I am, but I feel like a stick of wood, floating on a current, going past people. I can see them, but not touch them, not feel anything at all. I like that numb feeling better than the crying.

My mom was beside herself. If I could have gotten better for her, I would have.

Then, after supper one night, when the last of the crimson maple leaves have fallen from the trees, Dunn arrives.

"The poop is piling pretty high at my place, Katie."

For a second, light tries to pierce that darkness that crowds around me. For a second, I allow myself to feel important and needed.

But then I realize how ridiculous that is.

"What did you do before I came along?" I ask him.

He looks at me for a long time. There is something in his eyes I can hold on to.

"To be honest?" he says. "I don't know."

And so I start going back over there. He doesn't seem so worried anymore about whether or not people think it's appropriate. I think he knows something that maybe I don't even know. There is a life on the line here, and it is mine.

It actually feels good to pick up poop. I've been sitting on the couch for so long it hurts all my muscles, but the pain is a good pain. For the first time in a long time, I start to look forward to something.

Of course, it's not just poop. What kind of crazy person would look forward to picking up poop?

It's the horses. It's being around those horses, almost all of them at least as wounded as me. Mike and I start doing groundwork together, again.

The horses bring me back, and I think Dunn knew they would. Because a long, long time ago, they brought him back from the edge of that dark abyss that is grief.

The thing about being with any horse, and especially a wounded one, is that you have to be *there*. You can't be mulling over in your head all the things that have happened and gone wrong.

You have to give yourself over to that moment: you have to immerse yourself in the twitch of ear, the movement of an eye, the tension in muscle.

You have to be totally present to whatever unfolds, good or bad.

That's true of horses, and I guess, maybe, it's true of life, too.

Chapter 19

A LITTLE BIT OF HEAVEN

THERE IS SNOW on the ground when I finally go back out there to that mound. The snow in Um Yuck is so different than it was in Vancouver. Even our little stucco box of a house looks like something off a Christmas card with the heaps of sparkling white drifted around it.

I brush the snow away from the ribbons. Some of them have blown away, and some are still there, but looking worse for the wear, faded and ragged around the edges.

I know this is how it should be, for some places are meant to be marked, not with a ribbon, but by the heart. In that place, a little horse whose heart grew way too big for his body runs without wheezing for air, and he never knocks over a single barrel.

Here is a question I ask myself sometimes: if I had known Lt'l Bit was dying, would I still have taken him?

I wouldn't have. What kind of idiot would leave themselves open to a heartbreak like that?

And yet now, with the worst of the grief, finally, behind me, I think of those last weeks with him, and the intensity of the way I experienced him in his last days with a sense of wonder.

I'm a teenager. Of course it is all about me!

But for those weeks, it wasn't. Our relationship changed completely, from a child running after him, halter in hand, demanding life be filled with fun and excitement, to something else. Our connection, in the end, was so deep precisely because every distraction had been removed. There were no barrels to run and no trails to ride. There was just me and my horse and clock ticking relentlessly in the back ground, making every moment we had shine with an unearthly kind of beauty.

I am able to see so clearly, on that crisp snowy day, that I was one person before all this happened, and I am a totally different person now. A year ago, I could not have even guessed at the terrible things life had in store for me and my mom.

But, now, as the chilly breeze lifts a corner of a remaining blue ribbon, I wonder what if it all brought us to this? Losing my home and my dad and then my horse, so underneath it all, I could *know,* even when the worst happens, worse than you could ever imagine, there can still be good. I can still be okay.

It's a good thing to know that because sometimes my mom's face, when she looks at all the bills coming in, makes me feel anxious.

And because my dad has been formally charged, and his lawyer wants me to testify *for* him, because he never did anything to me. I talked to my dad on the phone, once, and he told me that the girl he thought he was meeting that day looked at least twenty. Which doesn't, in my mind, make it any better, and is different than the first story he told. Now, my dad wants to see me, and I don't know what to think about that.

He seems to have landed on his feet: he's selling high end cars now. He never even had to move out of the condo, because Grandma and Grandpa Lemon helped him—but not us—through the hard time.

Grandma Lemon still phones and screams at my mom, and even though it makes me feel kind of mad at her, I kind of get it, too. I understand she loves my dad the way my mom loves me. Unconditionally. Always. Grandma Lemon will believe the best of my dad, even in the face of evidence to the contrary, because that's what moms do.

Dunn thinks it's time for me to get a new horse, but so far I haven't wanted to. Yesterday he asked me to start riding Eclipse, but I know what will happen the second I get on her, and I am not ready to give my heart away again, just yet.

Standing here, with the cold winter air tingling on my skin, I understand there will be days, again, when I will win blue ribbons, when I will say yes to life, instead of no.

And threaded through those blue ribbon days, will be plenty of the other kind, where for the life of me, I won't know how to catch the horse.

There will be days when I lay on my back looking up at the sky and feeling ridiculously happy about nothing at all.

And there will be days when, despite the sun shining, and new adventures waiting, I will feel as black as though I have gone down into a seam of coal.

For all the terrible things, it's weird, but sometimes I feel better than I did before. Maybe better is the wrong way to put it. It is as if I have become, in the last months of my life, closer to being who I really am.

Stronger than I would have believed. Sure of who really loves me, and accepting of the flaws of the rest.

I guess I've learned that's life, some good and some bad, and if you can use the bad to become fully yourself? To have that quality of *heart*, that the old cowboys admire so much?

Dunn would call that a good trade.

A LITTLE BIT OF HEAVEN:

I'M DUNN

A Mini Book Bonus to
A LITTLE BIT OF HEAVEN

by
Collette Caron

Chapter 1

DUNN RIGHT

I'M DUNN, AND despite that stupid sign that used to be at the entrance to town, I really don't have any claim to fame. I'm not good looking. I was never good in school. I'm not good with words. I've never been rich or particularly talented at anything.

Except horses.

They are my one gift. I'm good with horses. I guess a man moves naturally toward his own salvation.

And there is no doubt in my mind horses saved me.

Since my wife, Grace, and my daughter, Emily, died—can it really be twenty years ago—I've had this weird thing. Don't get me wrong, I don't believe in any of that woo-hoo stuff like angels or auras.

But still, I have this weird thing. When I look at a horse I can tell just how broken it is. I can tell if there's any hope at all. Beyond the glazed look, the dejected hang of a head, that stench of terror that some of them carry, I can see something. It's like a faint spark that flares, for a fraction of a second, deep within them. It's not in their eye. It's in their heart.

So, there you have it, the one thing I get right, my one gift: I can see a horse's heart.

But I've never been able to see people's before.

Not until those two young women showed up at my place. At first, when I caught a glimpse of them, standing there in my yard, I thought they were sisters. But when I approached them, it was obvious the older one was the mother.

There was something fierce in her, like a mama bear protecting her cub. They weren't touching each other, in fact the daughter was mad as hell at her mom and you could tell that from the way she was standing. But that mama's fierceness couldn't be repelled by a little bit of mad, it was wrapped around that little girl like a shield.

I'm basically pretty insensitive to people, so nothing surprised me more than knowing about them, the same way I know about horses.

That something had hurt them both bad, and that they were teetering on the edge of a decision whether it was going to spiral them into a complete life catastrophe or whether they were going to be able to turn it around. Especially that young one. Some secret sorrow was eating her from the inside out.

But then I saw it in her, just the way I see it in horses. For a blink in time, I see the spark of resilience and strength and spirit. Heart, we old horse guys call it, in either a man or a beast, and it is, basically, the ability to rise above, that extra little bit of try, that refusal to be crushed.

So Mama Bear tells me they are looking for a horse for the girl, and it's like I wanna say to her, lady, pull your head out of your you-know-where. That ain't gonna fix what's going on here. I can tell she knows nothing about owning a horse.

But when I look at that girl, I think maybe. 'Cause look at what horses have done for me.

Plus, when Mama Bear tells me the truth, that she knows nothing about horses, I can't help but respect that kind of honesty. Because I've heard it all and it basically boils down to exactly what I said to them that day: anybody who has watched three episodes of Bonanza considers themselves a certified expert on every darn thing about horses.

You'd think people would be a little more careful lying, either to themselves or to me or to both, about something that can end you up dead, but nope. Women, in particular, seem determined to hold onto Black Beauty romantic notions, and are desperate to buy an animal that is way above what their skill level qualifies them to own. I avoid those types like the plague. I'm not having anybody end up in a wheelchair, blinking once for yes, and twice for no, because of a horse I sold them.

Anyway, I could tell Mama Bear and her cub didn't even have a passing notion of what Bonanza was, and boy, did that make me feel old and worn right out.

When the mom told me her budget, it was like Jumpin' Jehoshaphat, because a good, well-trained horse, that is kid-safe, is worth its weight in gold, and most people who have a horse like that know its value.

Anyway, being the hopeless optimist that I am—for those of you who don't know me yet, that is sarcasm at its finest—I say I'll find them a horse.

I already know there's only one place I'm going to find a horse in that price range, and chances of finding what I need right when I need it are probably slim to none.

Old Hank Charbonneau has made himself a pretty good business driving the meat wagon. He has a circuit all through Western Canada, picking up horses and delivering them to Fort Macleod, where they are slaughtered and end up as steak on some Dutchman's plate.

I'm not sentimental about horses going for meat. So many of them have had so much of the wrong stuff done to them that they are unsalvageable, pet pollution, pure and simple. There's almost as many reasons as there are horses that they end up heading toward that fate: old, lame, crippled, sick, but more often spoiled beyond redemption, unpredictable, mean, malicious and downright dangerous. Sometimes Hank knows a bit of the story behind a horse, and sometimes he doesn't.

His two-week circuit takes him by my place every second Wednesday, and he always stops in. We let the whole cargo off for a stretch and some water, and I look them over. If I take a hankering to one or two, or three, or a dozen, he'll sell them to me for a little less than the going per pound price that he gets at Fort Mac. I think, despite what he does for a living, he's got a soft spot for horses.

I actually prefer not to hear the story, if he knows it, until after I've made my decision about whether or not I'm going to take a horse. Sometimes knowing a horse kicked a man's head in will interfere with my ability to see its heart.

The black mare, it turns out, did exactly that. She bucked a man off, and then gave him a solid kick in the head, after, for good measure. It won't be the first time I've picked up a horse that is explosive, though usually once I start working with them, I can clearly see it ain't about the horse.

But Hank doesn't know anything about the homely little horse, except his name. The horse really is just about the ugliest one I've ever seen, but I learned a long, long time ago to ignore the outer shell of a horse. The beautiful ones can be hiding a dastardly nature, and the ugly ones can be sweet and willing. Come to think of it, it can be the same way with people.

Anyway, there's something about that little horse that I like. Despite his size, and his age, and his ugliness, he seems to have a spunky sense of himself. He's hard to catch, but in a kind of endearing way, like okay, buddy, what's in it for me?

I use oats to get a halter on him, and I run my hands all over him, looking for the flinching that would tell me he's got sore spots, but he only seems to enjoy my handling of him, like he's lucked into an unexpected massage.

I put him through some paces in the round corral. I can tell he's had a lot of the right things done to him. I'm a little too big to ride him, but I do, anyway, with my feet nearly dragging on the ground, and I am pleasantly surprised by how game he is and how good his manners are.

He doesn't have much in the way of fine tuning, he doesn't work off the leg, for instance, or change lead on command, but he seems sensitive to pressure and has the ability to find the correct lead naturally.

If I were to guess I'd say, from his size and how he hates to get caught, that he was a kid's horse and that someone has spent a bit of time with him, and that's he has been a safe, reliable, mostly fun—and occasionally aggravating—little horse for them who was probably hell on wheels to try and catch.

Except for that part—and she might as well find out now life is never perfect—he's exactly what we are looking for, for Katie Wilson. If I believed in them, which I don't, I might be tempted to call it a miracle.

I notice he has shoes on, and that they look fairly new, not worn down at all, and that gives me pause. Who spends a hundred bucks or more getting a horse shod that they are about to ship for meat prices?

I call Doc Johannsen out for a farm call, to have a look at the mare and Lt'l Bit, and she pronounces them both sound. I get the irony, now, of course, that I claim to be a man who can see the heart of a horse, and I completely missed the fact Lt'l Bit's was close to exploding inside his chest.

Chapter 2

DUNN IN

IT GIVES ME a bit of comfort that the vet missed Lt'l Bit's heart problem, too. Maybe, sometimes, it's the things that go sideways, not at all the way we planned, that are the very things that lead us to where we are supposed to be.

Her mother wouldn't know if the little horse was a mule, but I can tell Katie doesn't like the look of him. I count on that changing when she rides him, and it does.

I can tell quite a bit about people from how they ride, and I like it that Katie is cautious, but not afraid, brave, but not showing the kind of bravado that could get her in whole lot of trouble. She sits the horse well, and her hands are really light on the reins. You can tell she's had a few lessons, but really knows diddly about horses; but still, when I see her with Lt'l Bit, I'm feeling like a matchmaker who has done pretty good.

I take the mom aside to talk business, and find out her name is Penny. She's a stunner, and if I am completely honest, I don't know if it's her brokenness or her beauty that puts me under some kind of spell, that has me stepping up to the plate in ways I would prefer not to.

Before you know it, I'm in this thing up to my eye-balls. I'm selling tack on a payment plan and holding

Horsie 101 class, where I'm letting Penny know the real price of owning a horse, which is tack and fences and outbuildings and trailers and hay and oats and supplements and medicines and farriers and veterinarians. I haven't talked so much in about twenty years, so you'd think I'd shut up, but no, I keep yapping away, tangling my life a little more with theirs by offering to deliver the horse, check their pasture and fencing, and find them a supply of hay.

I deliver the horse and get out of there with my life intact. Despite the fact I have spent a surprisingly pleasant hour with Penny fixing fences that are falling down, I have come to the very important realization that I am way too old for her, and even if I wasn't, that she is way too wounded for me. I know how wounded she is because of all the things she doesn't talk about, as if her and that girl were born yesterday, and placed here in this town fully formed, with nothing at all behind them.

Still, if I thought I was going to untangle myself from them, when I see the state of their pasture I know I'm not, because the grass isn't all that good, and unless we get a passel of rain, they are going to be feeding hay sooner than they think.

Plus, Katie figures out pretty quick she's got herself a little horse who doesn't love her quite the way they show it in the movies. But I admire her for getting off the bus at my place and talking to me about it, because I was expecting she'd run to her mama and I'd get a hysterical call from Penny.

I give her the "flaws" talk which I have given about a thousand and one times before, and which is probably the truest thing I know.

I don't tell her what to do about not being able to

catch her horse, and I don't offer her a ride home, either, because you're never too young to learn that life hands you all kinds of problems, big and small, and you gotta figure them out. Really, if you look at it, that is life, you get up in the morning and figure out what to do about today's set of problems. No need to worry them too much, 'cause they'll be a brand-new set to take their place tomorrow.

In the thankfulness department, I'm glad, these days, most of my problems have to do with horses.

Katie doesn't come back and Penny doesn't call me demanding a refund on Lt'l Bit, so I figure Katie is getting a few clicks in on that life long journey that is horsemanship.

The next time I see them, though, is to deliver some hay, and it's obvious to me Katie has been crying. I know better than to ask—sheesh, is there a worse person than me to deal with tears issues—but I can't seem to harden my heart the way I'd like to.

Like I said, want to or not, I seem to be "in" this thing up to my eyeballs.

Katie asks me if I know what a Chester Catcher is, and I sure as heck don't, but I figure if she wants to, when she's ready, she'll tell me. Course, I can tell it's not gonna be good, so I am kind of hoping to go through the rest of my life not knowing that.

I end up picking up burnt cookies off the grass. Now, let me tell you something, you can tell by the gloss in her hair and on her fingernails, by the way every single thing she puts on, even sweat pants, looks like it cost a million dollars, that Penny ain't no cookie baker.

And she ain't. Even if those cookies weren't burnt black, she's missed something important in them. Possibly the sugar.

But as soon as I bite into one, it's as if the spell those girls are winding around me deepens. I can't get enough of those cookies. I have a pile of them on the truck seat beside me by the time I head for home, and I eat every one of them before I pull into my own driveway.

The next time I see Katie is at gymkhana. I can't seem to stay away from anything going on that's got horses and people in it. I like watching, dissecting, figuring out how they are communicating with each other. I like learning things that will make me more useful to my horses.

Lt'l Bit gets all excited and loses his mind for the barrels, and I can tell Katie is devastated, like she expects herself and that little horse to be perfect first time out, so I make a point of going and telling her to cut herself some slack.

They pull together real good for the last few events and I feel real proud of her. But then she comes and sits with me after, and shows me the videos, and that damned phone rings.

And I find out what a Chester Catcher is, whether I want to or not. Probably because of the damn cookies putting a spell on me, I feel like somehow I have to help this poor kid navigate through this really bad situation she's in.

The truth is, in my younger days, I would have wanted to gather a posse, hunt that man down and string him up.

But after Grace and Emily died, I had to do battle with my own desire to drown all that misery, and that battle humbled me and mellowed me. Over the years, I've come to see that it is pain that begets pain. And the only other thing I know for sure, besides the bit of wisdom about flaws, is exactly what I say to her about there being a bit of bad in the best of us, and a bit of good in the worst of us.

That ain't even my own wisdom, comes from years of sitting in rooms with other people who have tried, unsuccessfully, to drown their misery. So, I fight my instinct to want to take care of it, and trust this brave little girl beside me to have what it takes to figure it out for herself. To my horror, I end up babbling away about Emily and Grace and that dream I have.

Only I don't tell her all of what I'm thinking.

Sitting there beside Katie, for the first time, I think I know why I have that dream, over and over again.

It is the time in life I had that very thing I was telling her about. I had enough. I had everything a man could hope for and more. And I never recognized it until it was too late.

That little pony that appears in the dream, Benny, lived to be thirty-five years old. I don't generally bury horses on my place, but I buried him there. I can't go by that mound without feeling a lump in my throat.

Chapter 3

DUNN LIKE DINNER
(OR COOKIES,
AS THE CASE MAY BE)

I AM SICK to my bones when Doc Johannsen figures out that Lt'l Bit has something wrong with his heart and is going to die. I was trying to help Katie and Penny, and instead I just brought them more pain.

But I could see, right away, the death sentence changed Katie's relationship with the horse. There is a story I read a long time ago. I am not much of a reader, and so I don't even remember what context I read that story in, but it was about the Percival and the Holy Grail.

When Percival starts off, he is all about finding that grail for himself. He wants the grail to serve him. But after life has beat him to a pulp, in other words, made him somewhat teachable, he asks instead, how he may serve the grail.

And that is Katie with her horse. At first, it is all about her, and there is nothing wrong with that. That's what kids get horses for. To have fun. To entertain themselves. To have glorious rides, and freedom, to win a few blue ribbons at the local gymkhanas.

But when she realized Lt'l Bit was sick, Katie rose to the shift in what their relationship would be like now: she made it about him. She got to know what every flick of that horse's ear meant, and she brought that knowledge to my place. I could see it in her when I started letting her work with Mike doing groundwork on green colts. She was developing a knack for reading a horse that she would have never had if she would have just stayed at the level where her horse was a large toy for her to play with.

The day that horse died, her mama came at me like gangbusters. For a bit of a thing, she packed a wallop.

I didn't really intend to hold her the way it turned out.

I just wanted her to stop hitting me.

And she did stop. And then she was warm and soft and drowning me in her tears, and my hard old heart ached with tenderness for her. It's wrong in every way. Penny Wilson is way too vulnerable and she's way too young for me, she's got a pile of stuff to deal with.

But even so, holding her, I knew. I knew I wasn't going to be untangling my life from hers and Katie's any time soon. I knew I was going to be there for them both as they got through this latest hurdle.

I've been done like dinner since I ate those cookies. I know I could fall so hard in love with Penny Wilson that I would barely be able to stand it.

I hope never to let her know, of course.

But standing there, holding Penny, I remember that dream again. This time I can actually hear Emily laughing. My little girl is sitting on that fat little pony named Benny, chortling with pure joy. Gracie is looking at me as if I got up ten minutes earlier than her to put the sun out in her world.

I guess what eats me most about my girl and my

wife dying is all the mistakes I made that I never had a chance to fix.

Katie asked me one day if it was me that ripped down that sign outside of town, and I just didn't answer, but she knew I meant yes. I could tell she wanted to know why, but I couldn't go there. When she asked me why I'd quit reining, I told her it was because I didn't like what the sport did to horses. Or to men. And that was a partial truth.

Here is the rest of it: I wasted precious time chasing something that wasn't worth the trade. I was never at home. Grace was like a single mother raising our daughter. We fought about it all the time. I had the audacity to see her as the selfish one, getting in the way of my dreams.

She and Emily died in a car crash, driving through a snowstorm, to get to a dentist's appointment in the city. He was a specialist who was going to fix a crooked tooth she had. Did she think if she was perfect I would finally love her the way she deserved to be loved all along? Did she think the flaw was hers and not mine?

I was away in California giving a reining clinic when it happened. I should have been there. She always hated driving in the snow. I mocked her for that. When I should have been using my strength to build her up, I wasn't. I was using it to tear her down.

I ripped down that sign Home of Dunn McLeod, Western Canadian Reining Champion in a drunken rage of self-loathing.

So, for the longest time, I thought the dream came as recrimination. We could have had many moments like that, but we didn't. As far as I can remember, that happened once, that happy little family time, Mommy, Daddy, baby, pony.

But now, the dream doesn't feel like recrimination, a life sentence I can't escape from. The dream feels like a promise. That maybe I can have a second chance to figure out what's important, and what's enough. That maybe, even an old fool like me, can understand what it is when it has landed smack dab in front of him.

I don't want to try and hold on to it, to capture it, that little bit of heaven. When it comes, I just want to savor it, to serve it, for a moment, for that breath in time.

And so there you have it. I'm Dunn, old enough to know better, and yet still believing, somehow, you should choose decency. That you should be open to what life brings you. And that you should choose love, even if it hurts.

I'm old enough to know better, but I still think the good will outweigh the bad, and that there will always be something to hope for.

About the Author

Collette Caron is an award-winning author who has written more than seventy novels for the romance giants, Harlequin and Silhouette, using the pen names Quinn Wilder and Cara Colter. A transplanted city girl, she shares ten acres with her husband, nine horses, a Pomeranian, and a stray cat who decided to stay.

A Little Bit of Heaven is her first book for young adults.

Questions or comments?

Collette would love to hear from you at collettecaron1@gmail.com or look for her on Facebook: Collette Caron, author.

Watch for other novels by Collette Caron: *Joshua's Angel*, coming soon, and the third installment in the Horses and Hearts series, *An Eclipse of the Heart* (spring 2017).

www.ingramcontent.com/pod-product-compliance
Lightning Source LLC
Chambersburg PA
CBHW030534130626
46552CB00006B/2247